Searching for Intruders

Stephen Raleigh Byler

Searching for Intruders

A Novel in Stories

WILLIAM MORROW
An Imprint of HarperCollinsPublishers

HarperCollins books may be purchased for educational, business,
or sales promotional use. For information please write: Special Markets Department,
HarperCollins Publishers Inc., 10 East 53rd Street, New York, NY 10022.

FIRST EDITION

Designed by Kate Nichols

Printed on acid-free paper

Library of Congress Cataloging-in-Publication Data has been applied for.

ISBN 0-06-621294-4

02   03   04   05   06   QW   10   9   8   7   6   5   4   3   2   1

For my mother, Grace

Acknowledgments

Thanks to my agent Barbara Lowenstein. Thanks to Dorian Karchmar, also of Lowenstein Associates. Special thanks to Claire Wachtel, my editor, for her support and enthusiasm. Thanks to Jennifer Pooley for putting up with me and for doing everything. Also, a very sincere thank you to everyone at William Morrow for all their help: to my publisher, Michael Morrison, to Sharyn Rosenblum, Richard Aquan, Michelle Caplan, Lisa Gallagher, Joyce Wong, Kim Lewis, Claire Greenspan, and Juliette Shapland for her special interest from the start. Thanks, too, to Meryl Moss and everyone on her team. Thanks to Steve Weaver for his friendship and farm.

Contents

PART II

Part I

U-Haul

The night my father moved away he fought his oldest son. The fight was close. My father was fat, while my brother was athletic and lean. My brother dodged his blows and at first it appeared he would even win. But my father got his shoulders low, got his weight into him, and rammed him to the wall. A cuckoo clock my parents had bought in Switzerland jarred loose and fell on my brother's head. The clock was sharp and heavy and it cut his scalp so streams of blood ran down his cheeks. After the blood, they hugged and my brother helped him carry his things to the U-Haul truck outside.

Roaches

That fall the roaches took over our home.

I call it a home because that's what we were trying to make, but we never made it. It was a fourth-floor, two-room apartment with no sunlight that, like most things in New York, we paid too much for. I don't know why we thought after eight years together—four years of marriage—that New York would do us good. We were both new to the city. Neither of us knew anything about New York or about roaches.

"They're back," I said one day when she came in from work.

"Who's back?" Melody, my wife, said.

It must have been hard for her to come home during that time. I was working part-time and taking a graduate course in philosophy. She was working full-time, counseling rape victims. She looked exhausted, which was how she looked nearly every day I saw her come home from that job. She was underqualified for it, really, with only a master's degree. The YWCA had hired her to do "short-term therapy" with recent victims—or survivors, as she told me to call them—of rape or sexual abuse. She was cheaper for them to hire than a psychologist and she did all of the dirty work. She got all of the pain and anger when it was fresh, but she didn't work with anyone long enough to see them make much of any progress.

She set down the leather bag that held her work things—the files and papers about her clients—and looked slowly up at me. Her eyelids and the skin below her lovely green eyes looked dark and saggy, almost like she had been crying. She still looked beautiful, though. She always looked beautiful. She had been told more than once growing up that she had what it took to make it in modeling. Instead she had chosen to take on the burden of other people's pain, as a therapist.

"Who? Who's back?" she said.

"The roaches."

"Why?"

"I don't know. You tell me," I said.

She went to the kitchen sink—which was practically in our living room—and picked up a damp rag that I had folded and hung neatly over the neck of the spigot. She rinsed it and wrung it out and started wiping down the counter.

"We've gotta keep it clean," she said.

I just looked at her.

"We've got to keep it clean or they'll come."

"It is clean."

"No, it isn't." She shook her head and started making some strokes over the stove top. She stopped at a little black piece of something that had stuck itself to the white metal next to one of the burners and got down at eye level to look at it. She scrubbed at it vigorously.

"I already did that," I said.

"This is *hors d'oeuvres. Hors d'oeuvres* for roaches."

She had this way of selecting a dramatic word and exaggerating it with her tone. I always tried not to take it personally.

"I already tried to get that up," I said again, but she kept scrubbing at the piece of burnt food.

She stood up and pointed at the black spot and looked at me. "It's a *feast* for roaches."

She ran the dishrag under the faucet again and squeezed it out on the range to moisten the spot she was working on.

"You see, if you don't eat, you die," she said. "Roaches are like people in that sense."

"Who's feeding them?"

"You are if you leave it dirty like this."

"I didn't think I did."

She found another bit of something dark and crusty burnt into the stove top and pointed to it. I recognized it as the spaghetti sauce I had made the day before, which had boiled and splashed over. "That's the difference between you and roaches," she said. "To you this is clean, but to roaches this is a *smorgasbord.*"

That evening, after we ate and washed the dishes, we mopped and scrubbed the whole kitchen area together. We used bleach and Lysol on the countertops and floor, and we took out all the food from the cupboards and made sure it was sealed. We poured the open cereal and granola into clear plastic Rubbermaid containers. Even the linguine, which we had used half a box of, we broke to make fit in a Ziploc freezer bag.

"Did you have roaches at home growing up?" I asked as we were sealing the last few things.

She popped one of the pretzels she was transferring to Tupperware in her mouth and it made a crunching sound.

"Why do you ask?" Melody said, chewing nonchalantly.

"You just seem to know a lot about them," I said.

She clicked the top on the Tupperware container and put it in the cupboard next to the Ziploc pasta bag. "It's just common sense, really. You take away the source of nourishment . . . and you eliminate the odor." She thought for a moment. "You eliminate the *stench*," she said.

That night lying next to her in bed, I wondered if, after we turned out the living room and kitchen lights, the roaches had come creeping out again. It was cold outside, but we liked to sleep with the window open for fresh air. I felt the cold coming in over our heads, and it made me wonder what the cold would do to them. I could tell from Melody's breathing that she was still awake.

"How do you think the cold affects them?" I said.

"Who's that, Wilson?" She sounded weary and exhausted again.

"The roaches," I said.

"I'm done for tonight. I'm done talking about roaches." She rolled over on her side and faced the opposite wall. "Can we please go to sleep now," she said.

I was lying on my back, and I turned my head to look at her. All of the lights in our apartment were off, but the street lamps from outside were leaking into the bedroom. The skin on her neck and shoulder looked soft and wonderful and I found myself wishing that this beautiful woman—my wife—would suddenly roll back and want to make love to me.

"I've got more important things on my mind than roaches," she said.

"Like what?" I said too quickly.

"What do you think?"

The week before I had pushed her to talk when she didn't want to, and she ended up asking me whether I knew what it was like to listen all day to people who have been "fucked in the ass by their fathers."

"I'm sorry, good night, dear," I said.

"Good night," she said, leaning back and kissing me on the cheek as a kind of reward for leaving her be.

I lay next to her for ten minutes or so trying to sleep, but I couldn't forget the fact that I wanted to make love to her and I couldn't clear my mind of the roaches. When I heard her breathing change and I was sure she'd gone to sleep, I got up off the mattress—we kept it on the floor without a bed frame—and tiptoed into the kitchen. I flipped the light on and looked quickly to see if any had come out. There were a few on the counter near the stove and I grabbed a magazine in the living room to kill them. I got one, a tiny one, so small I couldn't even hear it crunch, but the bigger, faster ones scrambled into the crack at the intersection of the wall and countertop before I could get to them. I didn't know then what I know now about roaches. I didn't know that it's futile trying to kill them that way. I didn't know that it's futile to try to kill them one by one.

I sat down on one of the ice-cream-parlor-style chairs we had bought at a garage sale a few weeks before. They were horribly uncomfortable, but they were cheap and we needed chairs, so we had bought them. There was so little space in the apartment that we kept them along the wall in the kitchen and then dragged them out into the living room when we set up our folding table for meals. I thought about that, about how small and uncomfortable and underfurnished our apartment was. We had no furniture, but we had roaches.

I got up and went over to the window near the stove. It was locked, so I flipped the latch and opened it as far as it would open and I felt the cold air rush in. I went back into the bedroom and lay back down on the mattress next to my wife, and I felt the cool air coming in the window above our mattress again. "Roaches can't like the cold," I thought. I considered the cool air in the kitchen and wondered if it would have an effect. "They're like people in that sense, too," I thought, pulling the covers up to my chin and rolling away from her to the far edge of the bed.

The cold air or the cleaning or something must have helped a little bit, because a few days went by without them really bothering us. Still, I knew they weren't gone, I knew the problem would have to be addressed in more detail at some future time. Sure enough, when I went to empty the trash at the end of the week, a bunch of good-sized adults scrambled out of the container and back into the recesses of the cabinetry. That night I brought it up with Mel. She sighed and said, "I'll tell you what, I'm letting you in charge of the roaches." She had that tired, end-of-the-counseling-day look again, but I pressed her on it anyway.

"I just think it's something we should discuss," I said.

"I don't have time to discuss it."

"We can't just ignore the problem," I said.

"Look, I want to say this as nicely as I can." She took a deep breath. "I'm working every day and my job is very stressful for me." She took one of my hands in both of hers. "You're not as busy as I am. Could you just do this for me? Could you take care of the roaches?"

I felt bad that I couldn't identify more with what she went through at work, and I wanted to show her I understood the pain it brought her. She could have been trying to make lots of money, but instead she was sacrificing herself to listen to rape victims all day. I loved her for that.

"Sure, I'll handle them," I said.

She hugged me and said, "Thank you, Wilson. Thank you."

I don't know how long it takes for roach eggs to hatch, but that must have been what happened.

I thought about having someone in, some kind of an exterminator, but I didn't like the idea of chemicals in our home. It seemed like we should be able to handle the problem ourselves. I guess I was thinking that Mel was generally right about keeping things sealed and clean, that over time the problem would go away if we kept food away from them.

It was the one night a week that we treated ourselves to an evening out. It was Sunday evening so the city was mellower, more to our taste. We rode the number 9 train down to a cute little bistro place in that quaint part of the West Village with all the quiet, narrow streets. We liked that area because it seemed so much cleaner and more romantic than the neighborhood where we lived, which had high buildings, dirty sidewalks, wide streets and heavy traffic. We had a fine evening and we got a little tipsy on a bottle of cheap red wine. After the meal we got dessert crêpes from a little stand we knew about and carried them with us on the subway. We were going to feed them to each other in bed.

Maybe they had been coming out after midnight while we were sleeping and we just didn't know it, but I think the eggs must have been gestating and somehow they all hatched at the same time. At 2:00 A.M., when we got in with our crêpes, it looked like the kitchen floor was alive. They were all over the place. We'd had some cheese and crackers and a glass of our own cheap red wine before we'd gone out, and we hadn't put any of it away. They were devouring the cheese and crackers and there was even one crawling up the stem of a wineglass. Mostly they were in the kitchen, but a few of the bigger, more obnoxious ones had wandered into the living room. One of them, quite a large one, had flipped over on its back and was trying to get itself turned over again. It was writhing and kicking all of its little legs in the air, desperately.

"Oh Jesus, Will, kill it," Mel said, incensed.

Mel had hustled past the kitchen and taken a seat in one of our ice-cream-parlor chairs along the wall of our tiny living room. I had stomped on a few in the kitchen maniacally, and now I stood staring at this roach on its back with my wife staring at me. She plopped our crêpes on our desk, and some of the slices of banana with Nutella fell out on it. She propped her elbows on her knees and put her face in her hands.

"Do something, would you?" she said, almost shouting.

I stomped out a moderate-sized roach that was making a run for the kitchen and then I honed in on the one on its back.

Now I've killed plenty of things before—flies and wasps and mice and fish, even small game like rabbits and birds—but for some reason I was having trouble with this roach. It was just lying there upside-down, kicking its legs and wriggling. It looked so helpless and pathetic to me. It must have known with the lights suddenly on that it was in trouble, it must have sensed the presence of hostile humans in the room because as I walked over to it, it started moving its legs even more rapidly. It rocked itself back and forth on its shell to the point where I thought it might right itself and flip over and try to run away. I knew by this time that the big ones are very fast, and I was ready for it. If it did turn over onto its legs again, it wasn't going to escape. I felt kind of silly when I realized how I was approaching it. I had my knees bent and my arms out to the side like a defensive back.

"Wilson, just kill it, please," she said.

I wish now that I would have just so she could have seen me crunch it, so she could have seen me exterminate one mercilessly. It would have driven home to her the fact that I was doing everything I knew how to do, that I was facing the roach problem.

But I didn't. I didn't kill it. Instead I picked up a newspaper off the desk and scooped it up using the newspaper like a dustpan. I did it very carefully so it wouldn't flip around to its legs and run off the paper and up my arm. I felt Mel watching me as I balanced it on the Arts and Leisure section of the *New York Times* and opened the window next to our desk with my free hand. I thought one last time about crushing it, but instead I flipped it out the window, into the cold, onto the sidewalk four stories below.

It sounded like she was going to cry. "Why didn't you kill it?" she said.

"I don't think it will hurt us down there."

"It's just the *principle* of it." She looked away and shook her head.

"He'll die from exposure," I said.

"Roaches don't die from *exposure*." She put her face in her hands and then looked up and squinted at me. "You should have *crushed* it," she said.

I stared at her for a couple of seconds, perplexed and amazed at the fact that we were arguing about roaches again.

"Maybe you're right. Maybe I should have," I said.

She glared at me for a few moments and then she got up and went into the bathroom. I heard her pee and I heard the toilet flush and then she came out and went into the bedroom. I heard her sit down on the bed and I heard the sound of her shoes plopping on the floor. Then, it got quiet again.

I went into the kitchen and killed a few of the little, newly hatched ones that hadn't been smart enough to clear out once the light had come on. I smushed them with a paper towel one by one. I was beginning to realize how futile it was to kill them like that, individually, but it didn't stop me. I was taking some kind of personal revenge.

"Goddamn you," I said out loud. I noticed that one I had already smeared into the counter was still moving a few of its legs. "Die, you bastard," I said, crushing it again.

When I finished wiping the smushed carcasses off the counter and floor with damp paper towels, I went into the bedroom to see what Mel was up to. I thought maybe she'd be reading or waiting up for me, but she was curled up facing the far wall with the covers pulled all the way to her chin. I went back into the middle room to get the crêpes. The banana slices that had fallen out on the desk had deposited some of their chocolate there, but I just pushed the slices back into the crêpes and left the chocolate where it was. I went into the bedroom and set the crêpes on the windowsill while I undressed, and then I picked them up again and sat up next to her in bed holding them in one hand. I had stripped down to my underwear and as I got into bed I brushed against the back of her leg and felt the roughness of her jeans. She hadn't even undressed.

"Do you want to eat the crêpes?" I said.

She kept staring at the far wall.

"I've got them both here," I said.

There was a period of silence and then she said, "Did you wash your hands since you killed those roaches?"

I looked at my left hand, which was holding both crêpes. There was wax paper around the bottom of them and my hands weren't touching the crêpes directly at that moment, but in fact my hands hadn't been cleaned. I sat quietly for a while trying to figure out what to say.

"No, but I didn't really touch them directly," I said.

"The roaches or the crêpes?"

I thought about the question.

"Either," I said.

I listened to her breathing and watched her shoulders rise and fall while she considered my answer.

"I don't want the crêpes anymore," she said.

There was always something to feel dirty about during that time and it had begun to take its toll on our physical intimacy. There was the sexual abuse stuff she brought home from work. There was the filthy overcrowdedness of the city, the tiny apartment. There was the idea of making love to someone who you weren't sure still desired you. But the night we had a roach sighting in our bedroom seemed, the way I remember it, to have the greatest effect on our sex life.

It was my fault, I blame myself for it. I was supposed to be in charge of the roaches. I had promised her that.

It was a Monday night. She had come home early from work because her last client had canceled and she was in an unusually good mood. She had stopped and bought fresh flowers, blue orchids, and she had set them up on our portable dinner table in the middle room where we ate if we actually took the time to sit down. She had tossed a salad and made the dressing herself out of balsamic vinegar and olive oil and thyme and a bunch of other fresh spices she had bought that afternoon on her way home from work. We made the pasta and vegetables together and enjoyed an unusually pleasant meal.

Afterwards she had taken a shower and invited me to bed with her. It was only nine o'clock. She went into the bedroom with only a towel around her and lit a candle and turned out the lights. She took off her towel and got under the covers with no clothes on.

"Come onto my side," she said as I undressed.

Now the strange thing about our sleeping setup in that apartment was not just that we had no box spring or bed frame, so that the mattress was directly on the floor, but it was also that it wasn't a real double bed that we slept on. It was actually two single beds pushed together to make one large one. We used a separate fitted sheet on each of the mattresses, so there was an obvious crack between us, right in the middle of the bed.

"Sure, I'll come to your side," I said.

This was only one day after the crêpe incident, which is partly why I blame myself for what happened. I should have kept everything immaculate. I had slept in the morning after the crêpes and hadn't worried about cleaning up the kitchen until the afternoon, when I'd arrived back from class. I had almost forgotten about them. They were there on the windowsill in the bedroom where I had left them the previous night until just before Mel got home from her counseling. I was still scrambling to get everything clean when I heard her unlock the door to the apartment. It was only then that I remembered the crêpes. I ran into the bedroom to take care of them. Some sticky stuff had leaked onto the windowsill, but I was in a hurry and I didn't wipe it up. I accidentally dropped them on the floor and they left a moist sticky area on the hardwood floor, but I just smeared it quickly with my shoe. I put the crêpes in the trash can next to our chest of drawers and stuffed them to the bottom. I took the crumpled-up papers and used tissues and everything out and then I stuffed them back on top of the crêpes so the crêpes wouldn't be visible. I had planned to come back and tend to all of it—the sticky juice on the windowsill and floor and the crêpes in the trash can—but I forgot and that stuff stewed on the windowsill, on the floor, and in our trash can for two days. Mel, of course, didn't know any of this when she took off her towel and invited me onto her side of the bed.

"Are you going to *come* or not?" she said playfully.

She took my boxer shorts off and climbed on top of me right away. She put me inside of her so quickly that I decided she must have gotten herself ready in the shower or else gotten ready just thinking about it.

"Oh my God, Wilson," she said.

"Oh my God," I said back.

"Oh my God," she said again. "Oh, *Jesus*."

She got off of me and moved over to the other side of the crack between the beds and crossed her legs. She started rubbing her forehead and shook her head.

"I don't believe it."

"What? What did I do?" I said.

I was still facing the window like I had been when she was on top of me. She was facing the other way—toward the chest of drawers and the trash can. She put one hand on her forehead and pointed with the other behind me, where the trash can was.

I pulled the sheets up over my waist and sat up and turned around and saw it there. It was on the rim of the trash can, just perched there, unaffected, staring down in. It knew the crêpes were at the bottom, obviously. It was either breaking from a feast or it smelled them and was pausing for a few seconds on its way in. The candle was on top of the chest of drawers above the trash can and, believe it or not, the soft flicker from the flame was making the roach's shell shine, almost scintillate. The light must have made it look much bigger than it actually was. It looked huge.

"I'm sorry," I said instinctively.

That was the first time I thought of using the full name. "That," I remember thinking, "is a *cock*roach."

I guess it had smelled the crêpes and snuck all the way in from the kitchen because I can't imagine that they were living in our bedroom. It was dark in the apartment except for the candlelight, so that must have been how it had the courage to come all the way in and why it wasn't spooked by our presence there. I dug around for my underwear under the sheets. When I finally found them, I put them on and went over to the trash can. The cockroach scrambled down in when I came near, and frankly, I was glad. I didn't feel like chasing it and crushing it. I just didn't want to have to do that, not right after having, or sort of having, sex with her. It wasn't really the roach's fault anyway. He was just acting on instinct. I was the one who'd left the food around. It was only his need to eat, his survival instinct, that had led him into our bedroom.

I carried the trash can out into the kitchen and dumped it out into the bigger garbage can under the sink. I thought about taking all of the trash outside right then—I suppose I should have—but that would have meant hiking down three flights of stairs and going out into the cold with it or just leaving it out in the hall, which would have been pretty rude to the other tenants. I left it under the sink and went back into the bedroom.

"I'm sorry," I said when I got back into bed.

She was rolled over on her side facing the far wall with the covers pulled up over her shoulder again.

That night I dreamed giant roaches came up out of the crack between our mattresses.

. . .

By the end of November, Mel was ready to give up on things. She gave her notice at work because, she said, it was just taking too much out of her. We both knew it was going to be over for good when the lease ran out at the end of the year. We had been trying to make it work for too long, and we had both come to some kind of an end. When her job ended the first week of December, she packed her clothes and rode the train to Reading, Pennsylvania, where she was going to live with a friend until I came home closer to Christmas. We had decided, though, by that point, that we weren't going to spend the holiday together. It had to start being officially "over" sometime and there was no sense dragging it on.

Somehow, I was left the job of moving everything out. In that last week that I was there alone I had started boxing things up and everything was all over the place. I had packed up our cutlery and dishes and I had been getting takeout every night. I didn't really care about the roaches anymore, either, once she was gone. I didn't know what I was going to do. I didn't know if I'd try to find a cheaper apartment and return to graduate school in January or if I'd take off for somewhere much cheaper and slower than New York, perhaps get a job painting houses or waiting tables. There were pizza boxes, Chinese food containers and beer bottles littered all over the kitchen and living room floor.

One night just before I headed home for the holiday, I ended up at a party hosted by someone from the restaurant where I had been working. I didn't know many people there comfortably, but there was one woman there whom I had chatted with once or twice at work and who had seemed unusually warm and compassionate to me. She saw me from across the room and walked over to me carrying a drink, smiling. We started getting along quite well. We laughed and drank and talked by ourselves most of the night.

Now I'm not the type to cheat, but it was basically over between me and Melody and she was gone and I was drunk enough that I figured there was no harm in having a friend back to the apartment for one more drink at the end of the evening. I don't even remember exactly how it went—whether I invited her up or whether she invited herself along—but I was quite depressed at the time and she seemed like a very compassionate person to me. She had big puffy cheeks with dimples when she smiled. She was cute and kind, I thought, and I was glad she was paying attention to me.

"Do you want to smoke a bowl?" she said when we got in the door to what occurred to me, suddenly, was not just my, but *Mel's and my* apartment.

"That would be nice," I said. "I haven't done that in a long time."

She took off her jacket by the door while I turned the lights on. When I peeked around the corner into the kitchen and saw what I saw there, I thought of Mel's lectures right away. "You've got to keep it *immaculate,*" I heard her say in my head. Of course I started blaming myself immediately. I thought, *Now that Mel is gone and only you are here to take care of the apartment, they have taken over completely. Now your life is really going to pieces.* I've tried to be objective about this looking back on it because I know I was quite drunk, but there were hundreds of them that night. Hundreds. I'm certain of it. They were all over the kitchen floor. They were crawling in and out of the pizza boxes, *feasting,* as Mel liked to say, on all the food I had left lying around. One monster had its face buried in a maki roll I had bought from the sushi place up the street. It had its legs braced behind it trying to get deeper in.

"You can hang your jacket here," I said, stalling my new friend and showing her the closet next to the door where we had come in.

A bunch of Mel's jackets were in there, including the old leather one I had bought at an antique clothing store for her birthday. I felt hurt, momentarily, that Mel hadn't taken it along, but I didn't have time to dwell on that for very long. I saw my friend glance at Mel's jackets, but she didn't say anything.

Fortunately my stalling worked. I had turned the light on in the kitchen and living room, and while we hung up her coat most of them went into hiding. I shielded her as we walked past the kitchen and she didn't notice anything. I stole a glance in and only a few of the most audacious roaches were still out in the light snacking.

We sat with our legs crossed on the living room floor while she got out her little bag and packed a bowl for us.

"So how long has it been?"

"It's been awhile," I said.

I had had some paranoid episodes the last few times I'd smoked and I was telling her the truth when I said it had been a long time. I had basically decided that I wouldn't do it anymore, but this was different somehow. She gave me the pipe and asked if I had a lighter.

"I think so," I said.

I went into the bedroom and got the lighter that Mel used to light our candle and brought it in. I lit the bowl and drew on it and handed it back to her. She took a hit and smiled and we passed it back and forth like that a bunch of times. The pot seemed to be doing peaceful things to me, the things I figured it did to people who smoked it all the time.

"Kind," I said, smiling and passing her the pipe.

"Nice, huh?" she said at the tail end of her exhale.

We passed it back and forth, smiling mildly at each other for a little while longer. I remember that it was very comfortable between us at that time, which might be why she didn't feel strange asking what she asked next.

"Don't you have a girlfriend?" she said.

It felt sudden and a little threatening to me.

"Yeah, sort of," I said.

"She was living here, wasn't she?" She looked around at the boxes of books and plates and pictures stacked along the wall.

"Yeah, she was," I said.

"Where is she now?"

"She sort of moved out."

"Sort of?" she said playfully.

"Yeah, I think she moved out," I said.

She studied me for a little while and then she raised the pipe to her mouth to try to light it again. She had the lighter above it and drew on it, but it was one of those childproof lighters and she was having trouble with it. I reached over and took it from her and as I did I felt the feeling of my fingers on the soft skin of her hand. I clicked the childproof clicker down and handed it back to her.

"Now try."

"Thank you." She smiled and nodded at me. "Thank you very much," she said.

She locked her eyes on mine while she lit the bowl and then she looked away and exhaled the bluish smoke and said, "What went wrong with you and her . . . if I may ask?" As she spoke, her head bobbed around and her wavy hair bounced in front of her face on one side.

I took another hit and held it in and looked around the room at all of the stuff half-packed in boxes on the floor. One of the boxes had a picture of Mel and me sticking out the top of it and I recognized it as the sexy black-and-white one we had framed and hung on the wall of our bedroom.

"I mean, whose fault was it?" she said, and laughed.

I blew out the smoke and took time to ponder her question to me. I felt wise and in control, for some reason. I felt like the woman sitting in front of me was patient and on my side, like she was willing to wait the rest of the night if that's how long it took for me to search for the truest answer I could find. She didn't seem to me like the type who avoided things. *She can handle the truth,* I remember thinking.

"Hey!" she said, but I kept staring at the boxes of Mel's and my things stacked along the wall.

"I asked you a question," she said, leaning forward and smiling at me.

It was very quiet in the apartment—it was after 3:00 A.M.—and at that moment I thought I heard some rustling in the kitchen. There probably was no sound, or if there was, it probably wasn't what I thought it was, but just then I was sure I knew. I imagined thousands of roaches *feasting* on the *smorgasbord* I'd left all over the kitchen floor and countertops and stove. I pictured ravenous, gigantic roaches nearly the size of my hand scampering all over the room.

"Cockroaches infested our home," I proclaimed. I must have said it rather gravely, because all of a sudden she looked startled and uneasy to me. I stared at her eyes.

"Really?" she said. She bobbed back and forth over her crossed legs and laughed nervously. "What do you mean?"

"We tried everything," I said solemnly. "We tried cleaning things. We tried exposing them to cold. Nothing worked," I said.

She laughed some more, but I just stared at her until she stopped and then I started talking again.

"For a while I reasoned—dark ugly creatures that they are— that they couldn't stand bright space. I thought, 'If I leave the lights on in the kitchen and living room at night, they'll stay away.' "

She nodded and smirked. "Did that help at all?" she asked.

"In a manner of speaking," I said. "I mean . . . it helped in the sense that it helps . . . to take medication for a disease for which there's no known cure."

She uncrossed her legs and stretched them out in front of her. Then she leaned back on her hands with her arms straight behind her propping up her weight and smirked at me again.

"Well, had you any prior experience with roaches?" she said, raising her eyebrows and attempting an English accent.

I knew she was making light of me, but the question seemed highly relevant. I took a moment to stare off at the wall and consider it. When I looked back at her, her eyebrows were still raised and she was smiling at me.

"No, we hadn't. Neither of us," I said.

I stared at her until she quit grinning at me.

"All of it worked to a degree," I continued, "but roaches have a way of surviving, of enduring where, if faced with similar obstacles, weaker creatures would succumb. You try to expose roaches, you try to bring them out into the light, and they find a dark space where they can hide, a place where they can grow to inconceivable sizes . . . and then when it's safe for them, they come out again."

"They come out and darken the light of your universe . . . the universe of your kitchen," she said, gesticulating.

I should have known she was still playing with me, but I thought she was starting to comprehend the malignance of cockroaches.

"That's right," I said. "Exactly. And the thing about them is . . ."

"Wait a minute, wait a minute. Hold on, hold on." She held

up her hand and shook her head. "Aren't they *cock*roaches?" she said, blinking flirtatiously.

"Yes, they are." I stared at her, amazed that she knew. "They are *cock*roaches," I said, nodding slowly. "That is the full name."

She giggled and I stared at her with a straight face until she grew somber again.

"This is what I was saying," I said. "This is the thing about cockroaches: The more you try to expose them, the more they hide and fester and grow. You can't see them, but you know they're there somewhere in what you think is your *home* waiting to come out and pollute it with their darkness."

She picked up the pipe, which she had set down next to her, and tapped inside the bowl lightly with the pad of her finger to pack the marijuana down again.

"But you know what's worse than that?" I said.

She drew on the pipe.

"You can't see them and you might think they're gone, but all the while, they're multiplying and growing into a much bigger problem than you first had. You can try to kill them one by one. You can sneak up on them and crush their shells under a magazine or book or shoe, but by the time you see there's a problem, they've already started festering, they've already started laying eggs, they've already started making babies," I said. "By the time you acknowledge that there's a problem it's already too late." I realized I was leaning forward staring at her and that she wasn't looking at me. She was fiddling with the pipe, trying to get it lit again. "That's the thing about roaches. By the time you're ready to deal with them it's already too late," I said.

"I need to go the bathroom," she said suddenly.

Of course I knew that she had been mocking me earlier, but I was believing in her. I was still thinking that in the end, she was the kind of person who wanted the truth of things. I was still thinking, at that point, that she was compassionate and that she was willing to go the distance with me.

"Please don't go. I mean, if you can stay with me on this, I'm almost through," I said.

She sat up and crossed her arms over her chest.

"You see, what happened here was the roaches came between us—here, in this apartment," I said. "When I tried to expose them they festered and hid. It was always me that was saying, 'Hey, we have a problem here and we can't just ignore it.' When I'd try to talk with her about it she'd say, 'I'm busy listening to people who have been fucked in the ass, you take care of them.' "

She put her hands in front of her like she was ready to get up and back away.

"I'm serious, that's what she said. She's a rape counselor," I insisted.

"Who?" she said.

I recalled how Melody used to tell me my brown eyes were convincing so I tried to use them to plead with the woman in front of me.

"My . . . ahh . . . ex-girlfriend," I said, lying. I pleaded with my eyes. "She counseled rape victims." This part was true.

She crossed her arms in front of her again and squinted at me. I forged ahead.

"So I did take care of them," I said, "or at least I tried to. But you can't wage war against an army on your own. You might win a battle here and there, but you're not going to win a war against something as vile and elusive and malignant as an army of roaches. You're just not going to," I said, shaking my head.

Obviously the marijuana was having an effect, but I felt I was onto something, that I was experiencing some unusual illumination.

"No," I went on. "When the roaches are in your own house, it takes both of you to confront and conquer them, otherwise some will remain, or their eggs at least, and when the two of you think you're cruising along having a grand time, you suddenly discover that they have been there breeding all along. They've been there hiding in the cracks, hiding in your trash, and when they multiply and return their forces are *legion*," I said. "They come back as *legion*, I can tell you that much. *Legion*," I said. "Do you know what I mean when I say *legion*?"

She pursed her lips and shook her head slowly. "No, I don't," she said.

"*Legion*, like from the Bible. *Many*," I said.

She stared at me.

"A *legion* of demons. Like *cauldron*, except we're not talking about angels at all, we're talking about something much darker, something much more destructive and harder to contain than that. No, cockroaches are not angels," I said. "That is, unless you think of them as *fallen angels*. That may, in fact, be a truer representation of their moral position in the universe, of their moral consciousness. Yes, *fallen angels*," I said.

I stopped speaking and when I did I realized that, without the sound of my own voice, it was disturbingly quiet in the room. I stared at her and waited for her to say something, but it didn't look like she wanted to say anything to me and, in fact, I wasn't sure I wanted her to because she didn't look, if she were to speak, as if she'd have anything remotely kind or compassionate to say to me. I wanted to believe that this woman who I had thought was patient and caring and desiring of honesty from me only a few minutes before was still all of those things, but she didn't look that way to me anymore. She looked annoyed and impatient. She looked disturbed. She looked like she was through with me.

I listened for the roaches in the other room, but I didn't hear anything.

"Do you understand any of this?" I said.

Looking back on it now, I realize what she said next shouldn't have come as a shock to me, but it did. It shocked me horribly. It almost traumatized me.

"No, I don't. I'm afraid I don't know what you're talking about," she said. She stood up and continued, "Frankly, I thought you seemed like a very nice man, but now all of this is weirding me out. Now I'm not sure what I think of you."

She walked past the boxes along the near wall and back into the bedroom where the toilet was. There was nothing for me to do but sit there, stoned, and listen to her urinate. It was dead quiet in our apartment and there was nothing else for me to hear. I tried to listen for the rustling sound of the roaches in the kitchen again, but I couldn't hear anything over the sound of this woman's pee pouring into Mel's and my toilet.

When she came out, she went straight past me to get her jacket from the closet. That was her mistake. I don't blame myself for that. She could have asked me to get her coat for her and I would have. She could have stood up and said, "Well, it's getting very late, thank you for everything, but I have to get up in the morning and I should be leaving now." If she'd have said something like that, I'd have gotten up and shielded her from what it was that she saw. I'd have protected her from the trauma of seeing all those roaches on the kitchen floor and counter, I'd have protected her from seeing those cockroaches all over everything.

"Oh my God, this is *so weird*," she said when she saw them.

She brought her hands up next to her head as if she was going to cover her ears or her eyes. She sounded as if she was going to cry. "This is *so weird, so creepy,*" she said.

I don't know how many there were. The light was still on in the kitchen, but it's very possible that by that time the roaches had lost all shame, that they had come out in the light, all of them. However many there were, she looked devastated. They must have been still eating the pizza crust and bagel parts and leftover maki roll, because, oddly, probably without thinking about it, she starting licking her lips with a horribly disgusted look on her face. She turned and looked at me and said, "No, I don't understand what you're talking about. I don't understand and I'm getting the hell out of here." She looked at the roaches and grimaced and then looked back at me again. "You've got problems," she said, shaking her head.

I'm not sure if she expected me to make it better for her just then, if she expected me to apologize or back off of anything I had said, but I didn't. I just stared back at her and tried to work out in my mind how it had gotten to this point, how it was that Mel was gone and this woman was standing in front of me in our apartment causing me to feel pain.

"No, of course not. You wouldn't understand about roaches," I said.

Little League

*My father moved back in again after one of his affairs. I was
sick. I was coming out of the bathroom when I heard the
screams. I heard a thud, I heard glass breaking, and then the
moans began.*

*My baseball bat from Little League was in the hallway out-
side my parents' room. I had propped it there with my dirty
uniform the day before. I picked it up and eased open the bedroom door. My father was on top, his naked ass facing me,
gyrating. My mother was underneath, moaning, blocked from
view.*

*I pulled the door closed without them noticing and carried
the bat downstairs with me. I sat down on the couch with it*

and thought through what to do. I tried to listen from there, but I didn't hear anything more. It was over with by then. I lay down on the couch and pulled a blanket up over my head. Soon, I was asleep.

Helper

My wife and I had been having trouble getting along again, so we decided to spend a week apart. I started driving west. I don't know. I had been on the road for almost two days at this point, so that might have had something to do with what was going on. I'm not really sure. What I do know is that when I saw him hit her, something snapped inside of me.

I stomped on the brakes, jerked my car into reverse, and skidded to a stop in front of the couple along the road. I threw open my car door.

"Let's go," I yelled.

I started toward them, waving him in.

"You wanna beat on something? Beat on me," I screamed.

When the man turned around I saw that he was much larger and uglier than he had appeared when I drove past. He had at least three inches on my thin, six-foot frame, and though at least half of it sagged out over his belt, I must have been giving him seventy-five pounds. He was burly, but his cheeks and head still looked swollen compared to the rest of his body. He had a scraggly beard that strayed down onto his neck. He had on white high-top basketball shoes, black jeans, and a black leather biker's jacket complete with all the zippers and a big tear on the sleeve. The leather jacket was worn and frayed. I figured that his relationship with the jacket was about like the one he had with the woman I had just seen him smack on the side of the face, that he had been using it and beating it up for years, but he grew desperate and violent at the thought of giving it up.

"Come on, motherfucker," he screamed. He pounded his chest with his fists.

The woman was seated behind him on some concrete steps that led into a deserted pawnshop. She had dark brown hair that looked like it had just been blow-dried, shaped, and sprayed with finishing mist. Despite whatever she had endured in the moments before I had arrived on the scene, her hair still maintained itself with tidy curls that brushed her cheeks and splayed out on her shoulders. She was wearing a lot of makeup. Her mascara had run and it gave the area around her eyes a shadowy, disturbing look. Like she was peering out from a darkness I couldn't see into or comprehend.

"Let's go!" he shouted.

He came at me with his knees bent, in a boxer's pose. His eyes bulged.

"All right, let's go!" I said.

I took my glasses off and shuffled around to the driver's side. The door was open wide and I hadn't gotten my car far enough onto the shoulder of the road. People were easing past and gawking with their windows down. I tried to keep an eye on him while I reached in and set my glasses on the dashboard—he was coming toward my car with his fists up. I yanked the keys from the ignition and held them for a moment in my hand. I didn't want to leave them in, but I didn't want to have to dig around in my pocket for them either if I had to make a fast getaway. I threw them on the floor.

"Come on," he screamed.

He beat both fists into his chest again and it made a hollow, thumping sound.

I probably shouldn't have been, but I was surprised at how fiercely he was reacting. I must have thought he'd have some shame, some tolerance for my rage in light of the fact that I had just caught him cracking his girlfriend on the side of the face. Actually, I had done very little of this sort of thing. Once, when my brother came in drunk, I had fought with him, but that was a rare case. Usually, I just got out of his way and let him rant about whatever was on his mind long enough that he passed out on the couch. Then I could slip out of the room without creating a stir or, if I was too pissed off to sleep, steal the remote out of his hand and watch what I wanted on TV. The fights I had been in were always with family or friends—people you could trust not to beat you to the point of death if they got you down. I had been in a skirmish or two on the playground as a kid, but those never amounted to much more than a glorified wrestling match. The fact was, I had probably only taken or thrown one or two punches in my life.

I passed my eyes over the stuff piled up in my back seat and scanned it for a weapon of some kind. I had a fly rod in its case, but that wasn't anything more than a plastic tube. Swinging that at him would be like trying to kill a grizzly bear with a .22. I had a tire iron in the trunk next to my spare, but he'd be on me before I dug that out. I thought of the Swiss Army knife I had in the glove box. Fortunately, I was just sane enough to reason that I'd have to be out of my mind to show the guy a blade. I'd never use it myself and it would only give him an excuse to pull his own knife, or God knows what else.

He came around the front of the car and stopped on the other side of my open car door. I could smell his breath through the open window. He smelled like a still.

"Why the fuck were you hitting her?" I said.

I wasn't about to turn and look at the woman, but I could hear her. She had begun to scream. She was pleading in a raspy, high-pitched tone—the kind people break into just after something gruesome or irrevocable has occurred. It reminded me of the sound my friend's sister made at her mother's funeral when the casket was lowered into the earth.

"No, Scooter, no!" the woman screamed.

The man stepped around the side of the door so nothing separated us. He raised his fist and lurched his body forward like he was going to swing. I flinched, put up my fists to block my face, but held my ground. I noticed his breath again and wondered if he was drunk enough that his balance would be off. If I surprised him, I might be able to knock him down. I'd have a better shot that way. Even if he was loaded, I certainly didn't want to end up boxing him. I could see I was quicker than him, but he was too big to hurt with a punch. If he connected on me, I'd probably go down on the first blow. I considered moving away from the door and bull-rushing him—driving my shoulder into his gut to take him down—but I heard the woman wail again.

"No, Scooter, no!" she said.

"Come on, you wussy!" he shouted at me.

I stammered. "Well, what were you hitting her for?" I said.

"Hey, it's none of your business, man!"

"Like hell it's not," I said.

He jerked his head forward to try to make me flinch again, but this time I didn't move.

"*No,* Scooter, *don't,*" she yelled.

I wondered why she didn't want to see us fight, why she wouldn't want to see someone take a shot at smashing her abusive boyfriend's face in. But then it occurred to me that maybe she wasn't screaming because she was afraid for him, that maybe she was afraid of what he would do to me. She had certainly seen him get violent before and she must have known what he was capable of—especially when he'd been drinking. Maybe she knew he carried a gun. Maybe she had seen him cut someone.

I was starting to think it might not be a good idea to get into a fight with this man.

"Look, if I see you hit her like that, I'm going to stop and check it out," I said. "You've got to understand . . ."

I knew the possibility of it working was grim, but I decided to try to reason with him.

"You'd probably do the same thing if you saw a woman getting hit," I said.

He just glared at me. He had a long scar that ran from the center of his hairline all the way to his left eyebrow.

"Wouldn't you?" I said.

It seemed like he might be pondering my words, like there was a chance he saw my point.

"Look, I don't know the situation between the two of you, right?" I said.

He agreed with that.

"But if I see you hit her, I've got to stop, at least—I've at least got to see what's going on."

He nodded and pondered, but then he grew angry again as if he had become suddenly aware that I was tricking him.

"She's a fucking bitch," he screamed.

I contested the claim, despite my not knowing her.

"No, she isn't," I said.

"The hell she ain't. She's a fucking ho!"

I disagreed with that, too.

"She is. She's a fucking ho-bitch," he said.

I told him I didn't know her, but I didn't think she was that either.

"You don't see what she does to me," he said.

He was still screaming, but the tone of his voice changed slightly. He was almost whining.

"She hits me all the time," he said.

For a man who seemed, at least on the face of things, as concerned with preserving his masculinity as he was, it seemed like an odd defense. I didn't want to buy into his manipulative lies, but I was hesitant to just contradict him in case there was some truth to it. Besides, I knew it would piss him off again, that it would put my own physical health in jeopardy.

He rambled off a few more sentences about what a cunt she was, about all the shit he took. If I had *any* idea, he said.

"Look, do you two love each other?" I said.

It was sappy and I wasn't sure where it would go, but it was all I could think of.

"Do you love her?" I said again.

He scowled, shifted his weight, and looked over toward the woman on the steps. He looked back at me and pointed his finger toward my chest.

"Hey, fuck you, man," he said.

I stayed on him.

"You don't love her, then, I guess?" I said.

He moved away from the door and took a step toward me. I put up my hands.

"Look, I don't want to fight you," I said.

He stared at me, confused.

"I don't even know who you are," I told him.

I tried to convince him that my not wanting to fight was something like him not wanting her to hit him, and that that was something like her not wanting *him* to beat *her* up. The truth of it was, I said, that none of us *really* wanted to beat or be beaten on, that he and I didn't *really* want to fight anyway. Though I wasn't really sure what I meant by it, I told him we were all in the same boat.

His jaw was still clenched tight, but he inhaled and exhaled a couple of times through his nose.

"You do love her, don't you?" I said, trying to sound non-threatening, like a good therapist, like my wife.

He looked off toward the cars that had stopped on the opposite shoulder of the road and his forehead wrinkled up. A maroon minivan with some kids in the back had pulled partway off the road and there was a line of five or six cars behind them, unable to pass. The children in the van had their faces pressed against the glass.

"If you two love each other, then you shouldn't be doing that kind of thing," I said. "You shouldn't be beating on each other like that."

He looked over at the woman by the steps.

"Right?" I said.

She had stopped shouting. He looked at her for a couple of seconds and then he looked back at me. His mouth and nose twitched.

"All right, man," he said, reaching out his hand to shake.

While we clenched hands I mumbled something about us both being reasonable people, but he started walking away before I was through.

Though the treaty seemed authentic enough, I was worried that he would turn on me again. I didn't want to provoke him by standing there scrutinizing his every move, so I got back in my car and watched from there.

He stopped in front of the woman and looked at her for a few seconds before walking on to his truck next to the pawnshop. While his back was turned, she flipped him off. You could tell she knew what she was doing with it. She braced her elbow with her free hand and exaggerated the upward motion.

When he got over next to his jacked-up four-by-four, I assumed things were all right. I started up my engine and began to ease away. But as he was struggling to climb in his truck, she shouted something I couldn't hear. He pushed himself back out of the cab, ran back over to the steps where she had sat back down, and raised his hand. She cowered slightly, but stayed hunched forward screaming at him. I put my windows down and listened. She called him a fat son of a bitch, said that he was just like his dad and that he never had a fucking job in his life. "You can't even keep your dick hard, for Christ's sake," she screamed.

He faked hitting her again, but she didn't flinch at all this time.

I found reverse and backed up. When he heard the engine, he wheeled around and came toward the passenger side of the car.

"You see what I'm talking about?" he screamed.

I put my right hand on the gearshift. I was ready. If he tried to open the door or come in through the window, I'd take off. I imagined him hanging on, swinging from the door while I accelerated and swerved back and forth to throw him loose. He leaned down to the level of the window and gesticulated wildly toward his girlfriend, or wife, or whatever she was. The corners of his mouth were caked with dry white spit.

"You want her?" he said. "You take her, then."

I stared at him.

"Go ahead, take the fucking ho!" he screamed.

He was shouting, but his eyes looked moist. He stared at me for a moment and then he started toward his truck, stopping every couple of yards to turn around and offer her to me again. Each time he assured me it was okay. I could have her as far as he cared. She was a cunt anyway.

After he got in his truck and started it up, I leaned over to the passenger side and poked my head out. She had already dug out a cigarette from somewhere and had it lit. I asked her if she was all right.

She seemed annoyed with me.

"I'm fine," she said.

She flipped her hair out of her face, rolled her eyes and looked away.

I gestured toward the guy in the truck. I was worried he'd come back and beat on her again.

"Should I wait here until he leaves?" I asked.

She glanced at me, drew on her cigarette, and looked away again. I shrugged.

"Do you need a ride somewhere?" I said.

"Look," she said, exhaling smoke. "Why don't you just leave?"

It was possible that she was covering for him, but I figured it was just as likely that she was genuinely annoyed with me, that she saw me as just another guy who thought he could solve problems by getting loud and making threats with his fists. She probably thought I was hitting on her.

"Leave," she said, rolling her eyes again.

I kept an eye on him in my rearview mirror as I started to pull away. I saw him get out of his truck and walk back over to her again, but I didn't back up. This time I didn't even turn around. I reached over and tilted the mirror on the passenger side so I'd have a view of them. While he was standing over her screaming in her face, she busted him in the mouth with the back of her hand. His head jerked back and he touched his fingers to his lips a bunch of times, checking for blood. I drove away.

A semicircle of sun was peaking out above the horizon and its last few moments of light spread out on the fields of brown grass. After about a half-mile two police cars sped by with their lights on. One of the people who had pulled off to watch had probably called us in on a CB or cell phone. I was lucky I hadn't ended up getting my ass beat or thrown in jail. I took my hand off the wheel and tried to hold it still. I gazed off at the mountains in the west. Most of the mountain faces were shadowed, but a few, the west-facing ones, still had sun on them. I stuck my head out the window and felt the cold air on my face. I breathed it in. I had learned to do this kind of thing growing up in Pennsylvania. If it got loud or violent at home, I'd jog out to the little finger of woods near our house and go in deep enough that I couldn't hear anything except for the birds and the wind rustling in the leaves. I'd lay down and stare up into the trees and listen until I forgot about what was going on at home.

I took my hand off the wheel and tried to hold it still again. I looked back toward the sunset—at the soft orange light on the fields of dead grass. I tried to think about how beautiful the landscape was, but it wasn't working. All kinds of things were shaking loose inside of me.

Limp

My mother had allowed us the dog against my father's will. When the puppies came, he took care of them. With my mother working late and the rest of us, he thought, asleep, he bagged them in a burlap sack. I snuck out of bed and followed him to the river in my underwear. After he held them under for a while, he let them float off downstream. I kept hiding in a bush until he was back inside and then I ran downriver and caught up with them. They hadn't sunk. I waded out and intercepted them. One was still moving inside, but by the time I dug it out and got it to the shore, it had gone limp in my hand.

Floating

This happened the summer after Mel and I first split up, the summer after our roach-infested New York apartment. We were trying to make it work again. The trip west had been my idea.

We hadn't fought since Ohio and we had even made love once since we'd arrived in Montana from Reading, Pennsylvania. The sun was streaking through the hotel window. You could see the dust in the air.

"Hey, why don't we float the river today?" I said.

She yawned, pulled the covers up to her chin, and rolled over in bed.

"What am I going to do while you fish?"

I watched her shoulders rise and fall with the rhythm of her breath. I scooched up behind her and put my chin next to her neck.

"We can enjoy nature together," I said.

She yawned again.

"We don't have any inner tubes."

"We'll rent a raft," I said. I told her about a place I had seen on the way into town. The name convinced her.

"*Rubber Ducky Rentals*. Are you serious?" she said.

We took our time getting out. We ate at a diner on the main street in town where I used to go a lot—the place with the flashing neon EAT outside. We shared breakfasts. She got an order of eggs over light with hash browns and toast, and I got the pancakes. It was almost noon before we got to the Rubber Ducky place.

I didn't mind the guy at first. He looked rugged, like he knew rivers and rafts, but he also had a kind of round and puffy face that took the edge off. His eyes looked nervous. They were a glazed, washed-out color of blue and they moved back and forth in a way that seemed to reveal more than he intended. He was balding with brown hair and reddish-tanned, weather-beaten skin. He was wearing a fleece pullover that he had cut off at the sleeves and some old wind pants that were torn out at the knee. He had them rolled halfway up his calves and he had old wading sandals on his feet.

"Decent business you've got here," I said.

He nodded and smiled.

"This your first season?"

"Yes sir," he said.

The place was new and clean. He had a map of the Yellowstone and Boulder rivers up on the wall with different takeouts marked in red. I walked over and looked at them.

"Looks like you have your ducks in line," I said.

Melody chuckled and poked me.

"Was the name your idea?" she said.

He smiled. Little dimples came out on his cheeks.

"It was," he said.

He invited us into the back room where all the boats were.

Along the wall there was a welding machine and a fancy saw to cut through the metal piping he made the frames out of. They had raised platforms on the front designed especially for fly fishermen. They even had the knee locks you use to stabilize yourself when you cast.

"That's great. Knee locks on a raft," I said. "I've only ever seen those on drift boats." He lifted his chin slightly and gave a little half-nod.

"Where did you get the idea for that?"

"My head," he said.

I pointed to one of the catarafts. "How much to rent one of those babies?" I said.

He looked at his watch. His eyes shifted nervously.

"How about one hundred bucks?" he said.

It was strange that he didn't just state a set price. It was as if he was sizing us up, deciding what he thought he could get.

"Is that how much it is?" I said.

He focused on something outside for a few moments. When he realized he had been distracted, he looked back at me.

"Ah, that's the noon to six rate," he said.

He went in the back where the rafts were and pretended to organize things while Melody and I talked it over.

"What do you think?" I said.

She sighed.

"He seems like such a nice guy," she said.

"Is it too much?" I asked. We only had so much cash for the trip.

She connected her hands around the back of my neck and pecked me on the lips.

"Let's do it, let's splurge for it," she said.

"Okay, let's do," I said.

"We'll take one of those twelve-footers," I said when the Rubber Ducky guy strolled back into the room.

He told us he needed some time to do the paperwork and set up the rowing frame for the raft, so Melody and I went across the street to a little grocery store to get some things for the float.

Once we had committed to the rental, we decided the day should be special. We didn't want to skimp on lunch. We got a loaf of bread, a few tomatoes, some basil, and two different kinds of cheese. She was craving some tortilla chips so we picked up a bag of those along with some locally made salsa. We didn't have a container to fill up and I knew we couldn't go out on a boat in the sun without water, so we bought a few bottles of that. We got a bottle of wine, too. We had come all the way to Montana from Reading, Pennsylvania. We were going to do it right.

When the price came up on the register display at the checkout counter I thought of the man at the Rubber Ducky rental place.

"What do you think of that guy?" I said.

Mel had picked up a magazine on display next to the checkout and started reading it.

"What guy?"

"The Rubber Ducky guy," I said.

She glanced at me and looked back down at the magazine. She flipped the page.

"What do you mean?"

"I don't know, what do you think of him?" I said.

She flipped the page again and it made a surprisingly loud slapping sound. She shrugged, looked up at me, and raised her eyebrows.

"I've got no problem with him," she said.

I let it go at that. The checkout clerk pointed at the price on the register. I gave her two twenties and she gave me a few coins for change. We had dropped another forty bucks on lunch.

When we got back with the food, he was still finishing up the paperwork.

"By the way, what kind of rig do you have?" he said when we walked in.

"Rig?"

"Do you have a pickup? Something with a hitch?"

"Why's that?"

"Well, you'll have to get the boat to the river *some*how," he said.

"We've just got a little Subaru," I told him.

"I can shuttle you, then, for a few extra bucks," he said.

"How many extra?"

He rattled off some things I didn't really understand. Something about pickup and dropoff points, about how they'd affect the price. He saw I looked confused, and simplified it.

"Not more than twenty-five bucks," he said.

I looked at Melody. She crinkled her nose.

"I don't think it'll fit on the car," she said.

There was no other way to do it. I shrugged. "Okay, we'll take the shuttle, too," I said.

While he finished up the paperwork, I picked up one of his *Rubber Ducky Rentals* pamphlets off the counter and looked through it.

"This is the half-day price you're giving us?"

He kept scribbling on the invoice.

"That's right," he said.

The prices were listed in the pamphlet. A half-day float was supposed to go from noon to six.

"We pay that even though it's already after one o'clock?"

He didn't look up from the paperwork.

"You'll be on the water by two. I'll be here past six tonight," he said.

I looked at my watch again. Even if we got in an hour late—at seven o'clock—we'd be getting gypped for an hour of rental time.

"Okay," he said, waving me over to his desk. "This says it's not my fault if you drown, and this is the credit card imprint, the deposit for the boat."

I started skimming the fine print. I looked up at Mel for a moment. She was smiling. She winked at me. I quit reading and signed the papers.

"And this is the rental fee," he said, sliding me an invoice.

One hundred thirty-six dollars and seventy-six cents, it said.

I looked over my shoulder to show Melody. Somehow with the shuttle fees and tax and whatever else, it had jumped another thirty-six bucks.

She was standing with her back turned, looking at the map of the river on the wall. She had already picked up a life vest and strapped it on.

"Honey," I said.

She turned around, tightened the buckle on the life jacket, and did a little prance like she was on a catwalk.

"How do I look?"

I smiled at her.

"Great," I said, and then I turned around and signed the receipt.

The Rubber Ducky man seemed suddenly upbeat. He rubbed his hands together.

"Okay, you folks ready to roll?" he said.

He had us drive our car to a takeout point on the river only a couple of miles away and he picked us up there. While he drove us further upstream, he told us about all the places he had rafted and kayaked. Class IV and Class V water, he said, all over the world. Australia, Patagonia, the Amazon. He had even lived in Hawaii and kayaked the surf.

"Sounds dangerous," Melody said.

At the time, I thought she was poking fun at him. In retrospect, I don't think that was the case.

"Not once you know what you're doing," he said.

A flatbed pickup truck with a dog on the back pulled out in front of us. He drove up beside the truck and leaned over Melody, who was in the passenger seat, and talked to the dog.

"Mmm, you're a good puppy," he said.

The truck pulled off on the shoulder and let us pass.

"So you guys have some experience in rafts," he asked, checking the mirror and switching lanes again.

"I've handled drift boats," I said.

"Oh, you'll do fine, then," he said. "Those are harder to row than these rafts."

After a few minutes his cell phone rang. He told whoever it was he'd be right there.

"You know what?" he said. He folded the phone and put it back on the dash. "This other group is off the river and I'm going to have to grab them real quick."

I looked at the dashboard clock. It was almost two o'clock.

When we came to the takeout where the people were, he told us to get out of the van. We waited there while he ran them into town. It was twenty-five minutes before he got back and by the time we got upstream to the stretch of river where we had agreed to start our float, it was after three o'clock. He pulled the raft off of the trailer and told us he'd see us around six. He spun out in the gravel as he took off.

We dragged the boat down to the river ourselves. We got in and pushed off.

"*Jesus,*" I said.

"*Jesus* what?" Melody said. She glared at me.

"Nothing. I don't know. That Rubber Ducky guy," I said.

"What's your problem with him?" she said quickly.

"Well, for one," I snapped back, "it's three o'clock and we're just putting in."

"Well, we paid this money. We're going to enjoy ourselves, I hope," she said.

She stared at me for a few moments, but then she looked away and didn't say anything else about it.

I rowed us out into the middle of the river where the stronger current would take us up, and I leaned back in the rowing seat and stared at the blue sky. I let us drift that way for a while.

"Well, we came all the way out here. We paid the money for this boat. I hope we can try to enjoy ourselves."

"You're right, of course we will," I said genuinely.

We didn't talk for the next ten minutes or so. I rowed back gently to steer, but mostly I let us drift along. Slowly, the beauty of the natural landscape seemed to dissolve the tension between us. As we came into the canyon stretch an osprey dove and came out of the water with a cutthroat trout in its talons. It was a gorgeous stretch of the river and we decided to pull off for a while. We stood on the shore and stared up at the wall of the gorge on the opposite side. It must have been two hundred feet high. It was wonderful. The late-afternoon sun was on the red rocks. Sharp, rocky crags jutted out from the face of the cliff. There were spooky shadows below them where little caves disappeared into the canyon wall.

Melody looked at me contentedly and then squinted up at the canyon again.

"Watch this," I said.

I screamed and my voice bounced up and down the river, back and forth off the canyon walls.

Melody smiled. She screamed herself.

"HELL-O!" she shouted.

We listened to her voice ricochet and disappear. She smiled again.

"Let's have our picnic now," she said.

I rowed us over to the edge and dragged the boat up onto the rocks. There was a nice flat area, a kind of beach with smooth rocks and sand for us to sit on.

"Let's sit here, in the sun," she said, taking the cooler out and setting it on the shore.

We dug out the tomatoes, the bread, the cheese, and the tortilla chips. I had put the wine just at the top of the cooler in a paper bag.

"How's the wine?" she asked.

I let her feel the bottle.

"Did it get too cold?"

"I think it's all right," she said.

I used the corkscrew on my pocket knife to open it while she nibbled on the tortilla chips.

"What about the tomatoes?"

I handed her my pocketknife and she cut careful slices. We didn't have any napkins, so she brushed off her leg just above her knee and stacked them there.

"You don't mind eating off my leg?" she said.

I smiled at her.

She sliced up some cheese for us and stacked it next to the tomatoes, a little higher up her thigh.

"We forgot cups, too," I said.

"Let's drink it from the bottle," she said.

She looked off behind us toward the brown plains and the snowcapped mountains on the horizon.

"What mountains are those?" she said.

"The Absarokas and the Crazies," I said.

"And the what?"

"The Crazy Mountains," I said.

She took the bottle out of my hand and held it up in front of her face.

"To the Crazies," she said, smiling.

She put the tip of the bottle inside of her mouth and let the wine gurgle in. I watched her lips on the outside of it. When she had finished, she handed it to me.

"To the Crazies," I said, raising it like she had.

I drank from it and handed it back.

She broke off a piece of bread and handed it to me. I took some cheese and tomatoes off her thigh and stacked them on my bread. The tomatoes were wonderful. Ripe. Dark red. They squirted in my mouth and blended with the coarseness of the bread and the hard but creamy cheese. Next to the cheese, they almost tasted sweet.

"The tomatoes," she said. She chewed and smiled. "They're so perfect, don't you think?"

I smiled back.

When we had eaten enough, we walked along the river with the bottle of wine and took turns sipping it.

"Let's look for nymphs," I said.

I kneeled down and flipped over a rock. She crouched down next to me.

"There one goes," I said. I pointed to a little bug scrambling on the wet underside of the rock.

"Look at him. What's he doing?" she said.

It had six legs, a two-pronged tail, and two feelers coming out the front, and its body was divided into two parts. I recognized it as something I fished with.

"It's a stone fly nymph," I said. "They crawl up on the rocks to hatch."

I had tied up some golden stone flies before the trip, so I got one out of my fly box and showed it to her. I explained how they mature from the larval stage—the nymph—and how when the water temperature and all of that is just right, they float to the surface, shuck their shells and fly away. She took the fly from my hand and inspected it.

"Look. Like one of those," I said. I pointed to a real golden stone fly hovering above the water right along the shore. I licked my palm so the fly's wings would stick to my hand and I snuck up and tried to snatch it out of the air. It was flying, bouncing around just above the water, and I missed it a couple of times, but I caught it on my third try. I brought it over to her and slowly opened my hand.

"This is what that is," I said.

She was still holding the artificial one that I had tied. She held it next to the real one in my hand. They matched perfectly.

"You tied this to look like that?" she said.

I nodded.

She had always seemed slightly annoyed that I liked the outdoors, that I liked to fly fish. Now she seemed genuinely interested.

"Why don't you see if it works?" she said.

"All right."

I got my fly rod out of the boat and brought it over to shore.

"Here," she said.

She handed me the artificial fly and I started tying it on.

"What's it made of?" she said.

"Feathers mostly," I said, trimming the tag end of the knot with my teeth.

There was a place about fifty yards upstream where the river bent and some riffled water fed into a pool.

"I think I should try it up there," I said.

"I'll watch from here," she said.

I walked upstream and stood there for a minute studying the water and planning my approach. There was a current seam just off from the shore that looked pretty good to me. I made a few casts on the inside edge, but I didn't get any looks. It was a big fly that was easy to see floating on the surface, and I knew I had gotten good, natural-looking drifts. If there were fish there, they weren't interested in my fly.

"I'm going to wade out further and try to catch one," I yelled back to her. She was standing on the shore watching me, but the water was rushing around me and it was hard to hear. I waved at her and she waved back.

I waded out in the faster water where I could get a cast to the far edge of the tail of the pool. There was a foam line there where the currents collided and swirled—a back-eddy, where the foam was actually moving upstream. It was the kind of place where trout liked to sit, a place where they could have relief from the faster current and still watch for food passing in the water next to them. It was a tricky cast. I had to throw an upstream curve in the line and keep my rod tip high so there'd be some slack in the line and the fly wouldn't drag unnaturally, but it worked. The fly landed gently on the water just along the edge of the foam. A nice trout slapped the surface and then disappeared back into the dark water underneath. I raised my rod tip and the line went taut. The fish was there. It jumped twice in front of me and then took off downstream, whizzing line off my reel. I waded, stumbling, to the shallower water near the shore and followed it downstream with my rod tip high. It leapt again in front of Melody and then took off toward the opposite bank. I palmed the reel to slow it down and turn it away from the rock wall on the far side where it would have a chance to tangle up the line and break off.

"It's a big one," Melody said.

I played it for a minute or so, tiring it, and then I got it turned and ran it up into the shallow section along the near shore where it couldn't run as easily. Melody waded out and stood next to me while I landed it.

"What kind is it?"

"It's a rainbow trout," I said.

"Does it hurt him?" she said.

She kneeled over the fish with me while I took the hook out of its mouth.

"The barbless hooks are easier on them." I worked the hook out of its mouth. "I'm going to let it go," I said.

I held it a couple inches out of the water for her to see.

"Look at the colors," she said.

I dipped the fish in the water so it could breathe.

"Have you ever seen one alive?" I asked.

She shook her head.

I lifted it back out so she could see.

"The colors are brighter like this when they're still alive," I said.

She squatted down so the fish was at eye level and studied it.

"Do you want to touch him?"

She massaged the trout's side with her fingertips.

"You can almost feel the colors," she said.

I nodded.

"It's like a rainbow," she said.

"It's a rainbow trout," I said.

I put the fish back in the water and cradled it there for a few seconds to make sure it was okay. I let the water flow through its gills to give it oxygen.

When I had released it, she kissed me on the cheek.

She put both arms around me, hugged me, and then held my cheek in her hands.

"It's so good for us to be out here," she said.

We didn't talk much for the rest of the float, but it was the kind of silence that was okay. She lay out on the front of the raft wearing just her bra and felt the water with her hands while I rowed. Every now and then she splashed some water up onto her belly and chest to keep cool. A few times she wriggled up to the front of the raft where I was rowing and touched my face and pecked me on the lips or the cheek. Things were going so well. The sun was warm. The river, the plains, and the mountains were so fabulous. I remember, while she lay there, feeling the way I felt when we had first started to date, eight years before—slightly nervous, but thrilled to be with her. I remember thinking that maybe she and I could make it work again, that maybe we had come out on the other side of everything.

After a while I started rowing downstream with the current to get us to the takeout more quickly. The trip was taking much longer than the Rubber Ducky guy had said it would and it was starting to worry me. The rowing was taking it out of me. My neck and shoulders felt like they had pins and needles sticking in them.

I felt slightly annoyed that the guy had misinformed us about the length of the float, but I didn't want anything to taint the good trip we were having. I didn't mention it.

"It must be getting late," Melody said after a period of silence.

"Yeah, it must be," I said.

I kept rowing as fast as I could. The sun was setting by the time we got to the takeout.

He was standing on the shore with his hands on his hips.

"He looks pissed," Melody said.

"At *what?*" I said.

He waded out and met us about ten yards from the shore. He grabbed on to the front of the boat and looked up at me.

"This is going to cost you," he said.

I put one leg over the edge to get out and walk the boat to shore, but he started dragging it in himself before I was out. I tried to swing my other leg down, but it got caught up on one of the oar locks. I hopped along on the foot that was out of the boat until I could get the other one loose. When I tried to swing it down, the movement of the boat threw off my balance. I flailed and splashed. I got both feet under me and looked up at him. He was shaking his head.

I looked at Melody. She was looking at him.

I got my fly rod off the side of the boat and picked up my pouch of tippet, leaders, and flies. I started organizing them.

"I've been back and forth from the shop three times," he said.

I looked up at him again. He squinted at me.

"Do you have any idea what time it is?" he said.

Melody was still in the boat. "No, what time is it?" she said, as if we were at fault.

"It's after eight o'clock," he said. He glanced at her, but then he looked back at me. His hands were on his hips again and he was hunched forward, staring. His face and ears were red and his voice had started to shake.

"I thought you knew how to row," he said.

I didn't say anything. I didn't want a big conflict with him. I didn't want anything to sour the memory of the day we'd had.

"You don't know how to row," he said.

I zipped up my pouch of fly fishing tackle and set it and my rod on the shore. He walked to the back of the boat trailer and started stripping off the steel cable used to drag up the raft. The spool clicked and hummed and the crank handle spun in reverse as he carried it down to the water and clamped it onto the boat. He walked to the front of the trailer again and started winding it up. He shook his head as he cranked it with both hands.

"You don't know how to row. I was watching you from the bridge. You're an amateur," he said.

I laughed and shook my head.

"I told you we were going to fish on the way down," I said.

He kept turning the crank and the front of the raft started to raise up. Melody had gotten out of the boat and begun gathering things out of the dry box. I tried to get eye contact with her, but she wouldn't look at me.

He walked to the end of the boat that was still in the river and pushed it partway onto the trailer and then he walked to the front of the trailer and turned the crank some more.

"It's going to cost you, that's all. Another half day and two more shuttle fees," he said.

When he finished cranking the cable up, he climbed up on the trailer and got the cooler out of the boat. He plopped it down and it fell over on its side. What was left of our lunch fell out on the ground. We hadn't quite finished the wine. It spilled out on the ground.

I was losing my patience.

"It's not costing us anything," I said.

"The hell it's not," he said, looking up quickly.

"You told us it was a three-hour float. You don't misinform us and then charge us for it."

He shook his head and chuckled. "It's three hours if you know how to row," he said, raising his eyebrows.

I just stared at him. He kept grinning and shaking his head. I noticed the annoying little dimples in the edge of his cheeks again.

"It's going on your credit card," he said.

"No, it's not," I told him.

"Yes, it is. I've got the imprint."

"That's illegal, of course," I said.

"No, it isn't, you signed for it."

I shook my head and chuckled myself.

He kept smiling, displaying his dimples, while he tied down the raft. "Yes, I'm afraid you did. You signed it," he said as he hooked on the last bungee.

I told him I'd dispute the charge and report him to someone, but he got in his car and slammed the door. He spun out in the gravel like he had when he first dropped us upstream. I wanted to do something else, but I couldn't think fast enough. I just stood there stunned by his rudeness as he drove away.

Our lunch stuff was spread out on the ground. The wine bottle was on its side and there was a dark spot in the dust where it had run out.

"He spilled our wine," I said.

The plastic wrap on the cheese had come undone, too. The cheese was covered with dust and pebbles from the gravel parking lot. I picked it up and tried to brush the dirt and stones off with my hand, but it was hopeless. I peeled the plastic wrapper off, tossed it into the river, and watched it float off. It caught in an eddy and hung there for a couple of seconds, swirling around. I stood there wishing a trout would come and take it, but none did. It swung out of the eddy and drifted off downstream.

Melody gathered up the rest of the food and trash and clothes and put them in our car. My fly rod and fly gear lay on the shore in a pile. I took my rod apart and put it in the rod case and I gathered the rest of the tackle up and put it in the back seat. Melody got in the driver's seat. I got in the passenger side.

"What did you do that for?" she said as she started the car. She was staring straight ahead, not looking at me.

"Do what for?" I said.

She put the car in gear and pulled to the edge of the lot. She kept staring straight ahead.

"Do what for?" I said again.

I turned sideways in my seat and looked at her. She checked for oncoming cars, ignoring me. She pulled out and shifted into second gear. She was squeezing the wheel with both hands, pretending to be preoccupied with the driving.

"What did I do?" I said. "That guy was trying to rip us off."

She adjusted the rearview mirror and looked at herself and then she readjusted it and pretended to look at something behind us in the road.

I sat back in my chair.

"Did you see him shaking, Will?" she said, finally looking at me. "He was terrified."

I leaned forward almost to the dash and stared at her, but she looked back at the road again. I wound down my window and put my head out to feel the air on my face and calm myself. I sat back in my seat and put my feet on the dash. I rubbed my forehead. I stared out at the river along the road and I studied the seams in the water where the different currents converged and collided. I thought of them rushing and swirling underneath.

"He's doing the best he can. He's single, over forty, trying to make a living." She paused for a moment. "He's probably lonely, trying to hold it together."

"What's that supposed to mean?" I said.

There was another pause and then she said, "He sounds like an interesting person to me."

"He's interesting. He's a ripoff artist," I said.

"I don't know what you have against him. You had something against him from the beginning."

We drove for a few minutes in silence. I watched the river through the window, trying to relax. But I just couldn't understand. I couldn't help myself, I spoke up again.

"Can I ask you a question?"

"Go right ahead."

"Why don't you *ever* side with me?" I said.

"I've been siding with you my whole life," she said amazingly quickly, as if she knew what I was going to ask before I asked it.

I stared at her, but she looked back at the road, pretending to be focused on driving again.

"You know, I'm really trying here. I tried to make it a special day for us," I said.

"Was it a special day for us, or a special day for *you?*" she said.

"I don't believe it, I can't believe it," I said.

"*You're* the one that wanted to float the river."

"I thought you wanted to float it, too," I said.

"Well, there's not much else to do out here in Montana, is there?"

"Now you're unhappy we came? You wish we hadn't come?"

She downshifted.

"Didn't you want to come out here?" I said.

She ran the RPMs up and then shifted back into the gear that she had just shifted out of.

"Didn't you want to get back together?"

She sighed and pursed her lips and looked at herself in the rearview mirror.

"We could have gone somewhere I wanted to go."

"Like Club Med, maybe," I said.

It was a destructive comment, I realized, but it had slipped out and I was feeling too hurt to care. I was hurt that she wasn't enjoying herself. I had thought that she was. I was hurt that she was so opposed to the idea of spending time alone with me in a remote, natural, beautiful place. I knew it wasn't just *where* we were. Getting back together had been my idea. I had talked her into it.

We rode in silence for a while, both of us stewing. I stared at the river some more, trying to calm myself again. I tried to picture all the beautiful trout holding underneath, behind rocks and in the current seams, but I kept picturing the Rubber Ducky guy's face. I couldn't help but feel like he was to blame for Mel's and my fighting.

"Well, stop me off here, if you would," I said calmly.

She looked at me. "Stop you off where?" she said.

"At the Rubber Ducky place."

"What for?"

"Because I want to talk to him," I said.

"What do you mean, *talk to him?*"

"I don't know, I just want to talk to him. I want to straighten it out," I said.

"What are you going to do?"

"I don't know, just drop me off."

An empty cattle truck passed us going the other way. We were coming up on the outskirts of town. She shifted down into third gear.

"Why don't you leave it alone? Why can't you just leave things alone?" she said.

"You mean like leave you alone?" I said.

She shook her head.

"I knew this wouldn't work, it's hopeless," she said.

"Come on, drop me off," I said.

"I'm not dropping you off."

"Drop me off."

"You need to cool down," she said.

"I don't *need* to do anything."

She shook her head again. "Look at you, look at yourself," she said.

I looked at my own lap, my own arms and hands, and shrugged.

"I'm not going to let this asshole rip us off," I said.

She shook her head slowly and held her eyes shut for a moment.

"Nobody's trying to rip you off," she said patronizingly.

"Just pull off," I said.

"I'm going to the hotel."

"Then drop me on the way."

She squeezed the wheel, ignoring me.

"*Please* drop me off," I said.

She kept staring at the road. I could see the Rubber Ducky place coming up on our right.

"Pull over, come on."

"I'm not going to . . ."

"Come on, pull off!"

"No."

"Do it!"

"No way."

What I did then, I hadn't known I would do. I had no thoughts about it until I was actually doing it and even then it felt like it wasn't something I had decided on. Suddenly it was just *happening* to me and then it was too late. Of course I had no business reaching across and grabbing the wheel, but all I had wanted to do was steer us into the Rubber Ducky lot to go and reclaim what he was taking from us.

She held the wheel and kept me from turning it. I yanked on it as hard I could from the passenger seat, but she fought me with a strength I didn't know she had. It was as if she found some strange physical power in that moment, as if she had the sense that everything that stood between us up to that point was riding on our struggle over the wheel.

We headed off the road at an angle. The space in the curb to turn into the Rubber Ducky place ran out and we were heading straight for a telephone pole. She wouldn't let go and I realized I wasn't going to be able to overpower her, to swerve us to the right of it. I let go of the steering wheel. She wasn't ready for that. The wheel jerked toward her and the car swerved into the other lane. There was a car coming the other way and we hit it almost dead-on.

I remember a few things right after that. I remember the bizarre, shrill explosion of metal collapsing in on itself. I remember looking up at the cracked windshield and seeing the fractures spread like a spider web connecting to a point in the center, where a tuft of my hair was stuck. I remember the engine hissing, the smell of hot radiator steam. . .

Mel had been wearing her seat belt, so she was fine. But the man driving the other car was elderly and for a few days it looked like he might die. Melody didn't talk to me much during that time. She didn't talk except to tell me that she'd told the police she'd swerved to miss a dog, and that my story should be the same. She kept checking in on the old man to see if he had died. Fortunately, he pulled through. I had a concussion and they wanted to keep me in the hospital for a little while to make sure I didn't hemorrhage, but they only kept me there for thirty-six hours. Melody bought flowers for the old man on my credit card the day they released me. She didn't buy me anything.

Our car was totaled and we needed to figure out how we were going to get home. We spent a night in the same hotel as before, and the next day we rented a U-Haul van. It was cheaper than a car because there was no drop fee, but we still didn't have enough cash for it. We put that on my card, too.

Neither of us spoke while we were packing up. Obviously I felt horrible. I didn't know how to apologize. I felt humiliated for letting my ego get into it. I had lost my temper and it had nearly cost us our lives, not to mention the old man's.

When it was time to leave, she hopped in the driver's seat. I was surprised. I had thought that she wouldn't want to drive.

When we came up on the Rubber Ducky place, she put the turn signal on.

"What are you doing?" I asked.

She didn't answer me.

She turned into the parking lot and stopped next to one of the trailers with a raft on it. The Rubber Ducky guy was inside. I could see his round face sticking up above the counter. He was on the phone to someone and he was laughing and gesturing. Melody turned the car off, grasped the wheel, and stared straight ahead.

I put my feet up on the dash and my face in my hands.

I felt her turn and look at me, but I kept looking down.

"You wanted to stop off, didn't you?" she said.

I didn't want to look at her, but I could feel her peering at me. When I finally looked up at her, I saw something in her face that I had never seen before.

It wasn't anger. If she'd been angry with me I could have dealt with that, but there was a disgusting paleness and deadness on her face that I had never seen before on any living human being. Her skin looked pale and cold, too heavy for her skull underneath, like it was pulling, making her eyes sag.

She had made up her mind. She was dead to me.

I remember the thought that came to me right after I looked away again. I said it out loud for myself, or for her, I'm not sure which.

"One day I'll find love. I believe that," I said.

She rolled her eyes, pulled out of the Rubber Ducky lot, and started us east.

Bunny

We came up on the rabbit sitting still. It was nibbling on clover tops and we were close enough to see its mouth working in rapid, circular chews. "He's yours," my father said. I raised my gun and got it in my sights, but I didn't pull the trigger right away. "Shoot the goddamn thing before he runs," he said. I shot and hit it in the hind end. The rabbit writhed and squealed, but couldn't run. When we walked up on it, I asked if I should shoot again. "Finish it with your foot," my father said. I stomped on it, but I didn't do it hard enough. The animal rolled and squirmed. "Here, like this," my father said. He pinned the rabbit's head with the heel of his boot and ground it into the dirt until it didn't move or squeal. Then he stomped on it a few more times to make sure that it was done.

Shooting Heads

I was back in my hometown of Reading, Pennsylvania, for a few weeks, figuring out where to go next. In the usual way, the restlessness associated with that place took charge of me. I felt unable to concentrate or focus on anything. I put my sneakers on and jogged over to the local high school to do some laps on the track. Fretz pulled up beside me in the parking lot.

"Let's go and blow up some heads," he said.

I had seen him the day before at the local minimart buying a frozen burrito and a chocolate milk. He had told me he was still coaching girls' softball and teaching health class at the local high school. He had never made it out of Reading like he'd hoped to.

"Do what?" I said.

"Come on, it'll be fun."

I did wonder what he was talking about. He didn't strike me as dangerous.

"What else are you going to do?"

He had a point.

"I'm jogging, I'm all sweaty."

He shook his head and wrinkled up his face.

"*Jogging?* Get in," he said.

I tried to open the passenger door to his beat-up Honda Accord, but the handle almost came off in my hand.

"Here . . ." He reached over and unlatched the door from the inside. "Stuff that shit in back."

There was a cardboard box full of open tennis ball cans on the passenger seat. He picked up the box and tried to stuff it on top of two others like it in back. Half the cans fell out on the floor.

"Damn. Here, push on it," he said.

I collapsed the back corner of the box enough that it wouldn't bother me when I slid back my seat. He picked up a couple of old McDonald's bags from around my feet on the floor and threw them in back, too. A few fries fell out and landed on the carpet next to the stick shift.

"You want this?"

He pretended to pop the fry in his mouth, but he tossed it over his shoulder instead.

"Why don't you put those guns in back, too?" he said.

I didn't really know Fretz very well. We had had a couple of classes together in high school, years before.

"Guns?"

"The knapsack."

There was a flimsy pack at my feet. I felt the weight and the shape of the pistols when I picked it up.

"Are they loaded?" I asked.

"Don't worry about it. Stuff them behind the seat," he said.

There was an empty Kentucky Fried Chicken box on the floor and I laid the pack on top of it delicately.

"What are we doing exactly?" I said.

"I told you, blowing up heads," he said.

He pulled out of the parking lot and headed south on Reading Avenue. The first intersection we came to was backed way up.

"Goddamn this light," he said.

He did a U-turn and drove us back into the high school parking lot. He cut across the sidewalk next to the science lab and we came out at an exit on the west side of the campus. We drove up an alley for a couple of blocks and pulled back out on Reading Avenue beyond the traffic jam.

"Over there in the side pocket," he said as we pulled back out onto the main road. He shuffled around at his feet and picked up a cassette tape. After he inspected it, he dropped it back on the floor.

"The goddamn side pocket," he said, pointing and smiling at me.

The cassettes weren't labeled as far as I could tell, but he watched me study each of them as I fished them out of the door flap. When I picked up one that was on the floor under my left heel, he asked to see it. There was nothing written on it, but he seemed to recognize it.

"Pop it in," he said.

He started swaying back and forth to the music.

"You like reggae?" he said.

"I guess."

"What kind?"

I shrugged.

"Well, like, who do you like?" He rattled off the names of a bunch of bands I'd never heard of.

"I don't know much about reggae," I said.

He turned the volume up and bobbed his head and shoulders back and forth to the beat.

"I like to make my own mixes," he said, shouting over the music. "Like this . . . Fretz is a mix," he said, moving to the beat. He slowed the car and sang the words out the window at a jogger. The jogger looked terrified, but Fretz kept bellowing Rasta lyrics at him until the guy cracked a smile. Then he sped off again.

We drove for about twenty minutes until we were well out of town. After a while we came up on an old gas station with a hand-painted wooden sign out front. *BLUE BALL GENERAL STORE*, it said. Fretz pulled in and parked us next to the only gas pump the place had.

"You don't mind if we stop here do you? I've got to gas my-self up."

I waited in the car while he went in. I was all wet from jogging and I was starting to get chilled, so I fished around in his back seat for a T-shirt. I found one with a strange caricature of a guy with frizzy hair and his eyes popping out. It smelled okay so I put it on and threw my wet one in back. It landed on top of the knapsack and I remembered the guns again.

Five minutes later when he still wasn't out, I went inside after him. He was standing in front of the deli counter in back buying a sub. He seemed to know the woman making it. She was dressed in plain clothes and had a covering on her head that looked like a white net. She was either Amish or Mennonite.

"You know you guys have the best subs," he said. "I've had subs all over the world and yours are the best," he told her.

The woman making the sandwich spoke in a kind of a German accent. Her lips didn't move much when she spoke and it looked like the words came from deep in her jowls. She pronounced her *W*s as *V*s.

"Well, we have the best sandwich in Blue Ball at least, we like to think," she said.

"Best subs in the world," Fretz said.

We paid and went out. Fretz unwrapped the sub and took a bite on the way to the car. The mayonnaise leaked down his chin.

"This place has the best subs," he said again, shaking his head and chewing audibly.

I wondered for a moment about him as a softball coach. He had a sleeveless T-shirt on and you could see where the rolls of fat in his gut began. I tried to imagine what he might have looked like in his playing days—softball-playing days—tight-stomached and toned.

He wrinkled up his nose and moaned. "That smell," he said, shaking his head.

A semi with a trailer full of pigs had pulled up and stopped along the road across from the store. We both stared at it.

"Swine," he said, taking another bite of his sub.

I noticed the flesh on his chest sagging out the side of his sleeveless T-shirt again. It looked more like he had a woman's breasts than the turgid pectorals of an athlete.

"It's terrible, look at those fattened things," he said.

The pigs on the truck groaned and squealed and clanged against the metal cages they were in.

"You'd hate to be one of them right now," he said. "Locked in those cages, in the heat."

He stuffed the last of his sub into his mouth and wiped the mayonnaise from his lips.

"Let's get out of here," he said.

We drove further south, away from town, and after ten minutes or so, we turned onto an even smaller road. It was paved but barely wide enough for two cars to pass. We went through a covered bridge, wound through tobacco fields, and passed corn higher than our heads. We passed a couple of Amish buggies and the people waved at us. One of the buggies didn't have a roof on it—a convertible of sorts. There was a young Amish couple inside and the young woman was snuggled up next to the guy holding the reins. It looked like a date of some kind.

"Nice ride," Fretz said as they passed.

We turned left onto a gravel road and drove it up by an old stone house. Two little boys and a girl were helping an older woman hang up wash. It was summer, but the little boys had on thick black overalls, drab purple shirts and straw hats. The woman and the girl were wearing dark blue and black dresses with sleeves that covered all of their arms. Fretz had turned his reggae back up and we went by with it blaring. He hung out the window and waved and grinned. They smiled and waved back.

"The Stoltzfuses are the best," he said.

We wound past the house and came up on an old red tobacco barn where a man was breaking a horse. He had a rope tied to its bridle and he was trying to get it to walk around him in a circle. He was also wearing purple and black—a purple shirt and black overalls—along with a beige straw hat and white Nike basketball shoes. He took a hand off the rope, waved and smiled at us, and pointed to the horse.

We drove past another old barn and then into a grass field. At the far end of the field was a dirt pile about six feet high. In front of it, someone had nailed two-by-fours together into what looked like a jungle gym of some kind, and there was a plastic Tide bottle dangling from the center crossbar. We drove the length of the field and stopped near the dirt pile.

"So what do you know about guns?" Fretz said, getting out of the car.

"I've shot sporting clays a couple of times."

He stared off at the strange jungle gym in front of the dirt pile.

"Just a twenty-gauge, I think, is what I used," I said.

He opened the passenger door and dug around in the back of the car for the knapsack full of firearms. When he had wedged it out from behind the seat, he carried it to the front and set it on the hood of the car.

"No, I mean guns," he said. He unzipped the bag and looked at me with his eyebrows raised. "Like for killing things."

He took a pistol out of the book bag and raked it once. I just stared at him.

"I guess I'll have to break it down for you," he said.

He took a second handgun out of the bag and laid it on the hood of his car.

"Ever worn one of these?" he said, reaching into the knapsack. He pulled out what looked like two belts woven into a figure eight.

"No, I haven't," I said.

He came around behind me and guided my arm through one of the loops. I found the other armhole myself, and he showed me how to strap the front shut.

"Your pistol goes in here."

He stuck three fingers in the sheath just under my left arm. The vest tugged at my armpits and drew my shoulders back, so I had to stand well-postured, with my chest out. It made me feel bigger somehow.

"So this is supposed to make you feel like a badass?" I said.

Fretz tipped his head and smirked to appease me, but he didn't seem amused. He had suddenly become very serious.

"That's right, it goes under your sport coat," he said without smiling.

When he had strapped on his own shooting vest he picked up one of the pistols off the hood of the car.

"This is your piece," he said.

He cradled the underside of the gun in his palm and kept the barrel pointing toward the ground.

"What is it?" I said.

"This is the Beretta 92F. It's one of the . . ." He squinted back in the direction of the farmhouse. "One of the best five or six handguns ever made."

"What makes it so good?"

He rubbed the top of it with his free hand. "It's been around," he said. "This gun's been around." He held the gun flat in his palm and looked at it soberly. "It's killed a lot of things."

"I see," I said.

"Now . . ." He showed me the underside of the gun handle. "Your clip goes in here."

"My clip?"

"This is a clip."

He pulled a clip out of the backpack and handed it to me. I inspected it. It was a rectangular piece about the length of the life line on my palm. The metal felt cold in my hand.

"A full clip," he said.

I could see a bullet in the slot in front. Near the back of the clip there was a tiny hole where the brass from the bullet shone through.

"You press here." He pushed a button on the handle of the gun. "And you put it in like this." He crammed the clip into the rectangular hole on the underside of the gun and then he gripped the gun a little more firmly and held it out at arm's length. He raked the top, let it snap back, and raised his eyebrows at me.

"Now there's a bullet in the chamber," he said.

He pressed the button on the handle and slid out the clip, and then he raked the gun again. The bullet that had been in the chamber popped out on the ground.

"You do it."

"Do what?"

"Put in the clip. Show me how," he said.

He slid the chamber shut and handed me the gun. I cradled it in my palm and pointed it toward the ground like he had when he was loading it.

"Go ahead."

"All right," I said. "You press this . . ." I looked up at him and he handed me the clip. "And you slide it in like this."

I tried to slip the clip in the handle, but it didn't fit. I glanced at him for help, but he just stared at me and chewed on his upper lip. I studied the clip and the hole in the bottom of the handle of the gun and figured out what the problem was.

"Oh, it's backwards," I said, smiling.

He kept chewing on his lip, staring at me.

I turned the clip around and slid it in the bottom of the gun. The sound impressed me. It was a shrill, but smooth, grinding noise. There didn't seem to be any oil between the clip and the hole in the underside of the gun where it fit, and yet it slid in naturally. It fascinated me—steel parts machined to size, fitting perfectly.

"Now?"

"Now you need to get a bullet in the chamber," he said.

I pulled the slide on the top of the pistol toward me and it snapped back into place.

He shook his head.

"There's no bullet in. You didn't do it far enough. Rake it for real once," he said.

I pulled it back further, but still not far enough.

"No, man, give it to me."

He took the gun from me and yanked the slide back violently. When he let go, the slide jerked forward, back into place.

"Just like in the movies," he said. He still didn't smile. "Now don't be afraid of it," he said, handing me the gun again.

"There's a bullet in now?" I said.

"There's a bullet in the chamber, but the safety is on. Rake another one in."

I ripped it back and let go of it. It made the same shrill, smooth grinding noise it had made when I put the clip in. I recognized the sound from TV.

"Stay there."

He bent down and picked up the bullet that had popped out when I raked it and he walked over to the strange jungle-gym-looking thing. He picked up some empty tennis ball cans that were lying behind it on the ground.

"That thing's loaded now, don't shoot me," he said as he stacked the cans up in front of the dirt pile. Then he came over and stood next to me.

"Now take out those cans," he said, pointing at them.

"You show me how," I said.

"No, you show me," he said.

I tried to remember what the people looked like whom I had seen fire pistols in the movies or on TV. I took a wide stance and raised my arms in front. I fired the gun and dirt flew up above one of the tennis ball cans, so I adjusted my aim lower and fired again. I missed. Dirt flew up below it this time.

"What am I doing wrong?" I asked.

He didn't answer me, just gestured toward the target, telling me to try again. I fired twice more, throwing up dust below the target both times. I gripped the gun tighter and fired a bunch more times, missing left and high and then right and low.

"Should my arms be relaxed, or stiff?" I asked.

He held his arms out in front as if he had a gun. He bent his knees slightly.

"Legs shoulder width, weight forward . . ." He bounced his weight forward onto the balls of his feet and closed his eyes to get the feel of it. "Arms fully extended, hands firm, but relaxed."

I tried to mimic his form and fired twice more, but I missed both times. I was getting annoyed, but I liked the feel of the gun going off. I fired two more times in rapid succession and then I pulled the trigger a third time, but nothing happened. It was the end of the round.

"I suck," I said, dropping my arms at my sides and looking at him, but he had already homed in. He had the other gun raised in front of him. He was squinting, his lips were turned down at the corners, and his nose was wrinkled up. He seemed not to hear me talking.

His first shot didn't hit anything, but on the second he corrected and the can on the far left flew up in the air. On the third, fourth, and fifth shots he took cans cleanly and on the sixth he grazed the side of one and it wobbled back and forth like a drunk man. His arms started to drop while he waited for it to steady or fall, but he grew impatient and shot it and sent it flying before it had the chance to stop bobbing back and forth. On the next couple of shots he took out the last can standing and he shot up one of the cans that was already lying on its side. Then he blasted the orange Tide bottle hanging from the rail of the jungle gym so it gyrated wildly.

He raked the gun once, pulled out the clip, and stood with his arms at his sides.

"That's pretty good shooting," I said.

He got some bullets out of the backpack, which was on the hood of the car, and started reloading. The lift gate was open on the hatchback and I sat down on the back of the car with my feet on the ground. I looked in toward the stone house and wondered about the children and woman we saw hanging up wash on the way in. The man training the horse had gone in and put the horse out to graze.

"They don't mind us shooting here?"

"They don't mind. The owner gave me permission. They rent the farm."

"Aren't they pacifists?" I said.

"We're not killing anyone," he said.

I wasn't sure how I felt about the whole thing. It was a beautiful afternoon. The horse was only a couple of hundred yards away, but, surprisingly, it hadn't spooked. Its head was down and it was nibbling on grass. The corn was high and green as far as you could see and there was a handsome tree line to the left of us—a row of oak and elm and different kinds of pine. The Amish were working peacefully. The sun was going down. And our gun blasts were echoing across the countryside.

"There are more bullets over here. I can show you how to load the bullets into the clip."

"I think I'm going to sit this one out," I said.

While he reloaded a clip, I considered again the fact that I really didn't know him that well. I knew him about as well as you know someone you're not close to in a small town like ours. We had ended up in the same bars complaining about our hometown. We had bought each other drinks a few times.

"Fretz, can I ask you something?" I said.

He took a wad of tissue he had been using as an earplug out of one of his ears and looked at it. He shrugged.

"Sure."

"When did you start doing all of this?"

"All of what?"

"All of this." I gestured toward the targets and the dirt pile.

"Shooting?"

"Yeah," I said.

He looked off at the row of trees next to us and focused on the top of one.

"Four years ago," he said. He put a bullet between his teeth and started messing with the clip. "It'll be four years in August, I guess."

"Yeah?"

"Yeah, about four years."

I waited for him to go on, but he kept fiddling with the clip.

"Okay, *why* did you start shooting?" I said.

He took the bullet out from between his teeth and looked up at me.

"Look, if you're not enjoying yourself, I can take you home," he said.

He put the bullet back in his teeth and started loading the clip again.

"No, it's just that . . . I mean . . . you're a high school softball coach," I said.

He looked at me confused.

"So?" he said.

"It's not something everyone is into."

"Softball?"

"No, blowing shit up on Amish farms."

The clip was almost full so the last few bullets were hard for him to get in. With one hand he trapped the clip on the hood of the car, and with the other he forced the last bullet in against the resistance of the spring.

"I used to hate guns," he said, looking up at me.

"When?"

"My whole life."

He walked to the back of the car.

"You didn't like guns?"

"I hated them." He pulled a wad of tissue out of his other ear. "My ex-wife drove me to them."

He stuck his head in the back of the hatchback and pulled the cover off the compartment that the spare tire was in.

"Where are those fucking things?" he said.

"What things?"

"Nothing," he said.

He threw a tire iron, a pair of jeans, and a couple of empty beer cans out of the tire compartment onto the ground.

"So she wanted the gun?" I said.

"Yeah, she was terrified."

"Terrified?"

"Terrified of life."

"Of burglars?"

"Who knows? Yeah, burglars, I guess." He threw an old towel, another shirt, and a couple of softballs out on the ground. "God-damnit, where are those damn things?"

"What are you looking for?"

"Here they are," he said.

He reached down into the spare-tire compartment and pulled out two heads. He held them by the hair, one in each hand.

"Jesus," I said, flinching.

He grinned at me. "Don't worry, they're not real," he said.

"They look real."

"They're just rubber," he said.

He swung one back and forth by the hair, underhand, and let it fly toward me. It came straight toward my crotch so I had to catch it. The face felt soft, almost like flesh, and the hair felt disturbingly real. I dropped it on the ground in front of me.

"You're scared of it?" He grinned.

"Hell, yeah, I'm scared of it."

"Made with genuine human hair," he said, smiling.

He tossed the other head on the ground at my feet.

"Now it's time for the real fun," he said.

I stared at the rubber heads on the ground in front of me while he got a briefcase out of the back and walked to the front of the car. One was a female, a brunette, with thin, delicate lips. The other was male. It had blond hair and high cheekbones, handsome angular features. Both heads were already partially mangled, apparently from other shooting sessions.

"So what happened was she was fucking one of our mutual friends," he said.

I noticed his high hairline and the little tuft of hair that ran down the front of his forehead into a point. A vein that ran past his eye and up under the hair on his balding head was bulging out.

"She denied it at first." He unbuckled the briefcase and opened it. "I mean, this was one of *our friends,*" he said, looking up at me.

I wasn't sure what to say and I wasn't sure what any of it had to do with him getting into guns, but I let him go on.

"I mean, that's not something you do," he said.

I nodded at him.

"I mean, that's just not cool."

"No, it's not cool," I said.

He took the handle of a gun out of the briefcase and started screwing a barrel onto it.

"You don't fuck your husband and your husband's friend at the same time."

"No, you don't," I said.

He twisted the barrel on a few more turns, looked in the end of it with one eye closed, and started twisting again.

"Do you?"

"No, you don't," I said.

He stared at me blankly for a couple of seconds. I couldn't tell if he was focused on my face or on something behind me in toward the house. He started shaking his head again.

"She was so fucking terrified."

"Terrified?"

"Terrified of life," he said.

He secured the joint and held up the gun in front of him.

"Sweet piece, huh?"

"Yeah, sweet. Where the hell did you get it?" I said. It looked like some kind of machine gun.

"Now this is a real gun," he said, holding it up and admiring it.

"A real one?"

He nodded slowly and smiled at me.

"The real deal," he said.

He looked off at the cornfield and seemed to think about something else for a couple of seconds, but then he went on again.

"So one weekend I told her I was going away with some friends. I mean, I'm not fucking stupid, you know?"

"No, you're not," I said, staring at him.

"I packed a bag of stuff and everything. Packed it the morning I was supposed to leave. I did it while she was getting dressed for work to drive it home to her that I'd be out of town. 'What are you going to do this weekend?' I asked her. 'Oh, probably some things around the house,' she said."

He stared at me and shook his head.

"Jesus fucking Christ, *some things around the house,*" he said. "Jesus."

"Fucking *Jesus* is right," he said.

He took some kind of clip out of the briefcase and jammed it into the bottom of the gun. With the clip in, I recognized it as something I had seen in war movies and news spots. A machine gun of some sort.

"Fretz, what the hell is that?" I said.

"My wife?"

"The gun, for Christ's sake."

He held it up horizontally in front of his face. "This . . .," he said, smirking, ". . . is a serious fucking piece."

He looked at me like he wanted me to respond again. "It's an AK-47. Four hundred rounds per minute," he said. I looked in at the house uneasily and then looked back at him.

"Is that thing legal?" I said.

"Don't worry about it," he said, looking off at the targets.

I glanced in the direction of the road we had turned off to come into the lane, and looked back at him.

"So anyway, I work a little late and around seven I decide to take a pass by the house."

I stared at the gun.

"And guess whose fucking car is there?"

"I don't know, whose?" I said.

"Whose do you think?"

"Your friend's?"

"Damn right."

I shook my head and tried not to be preoccupied with the gun. "Then what did you do?" I said, glancing in at the house again.

"I went to the bar. I went to Sal's and did a couple of shots of J.D., that's what I did. I bought this guy at the bar a round to do with me and told him about it. 'My wife is fucking one of my good friends. She's probably down on him right now—while we drink this,' I told him. The guy drank it and slammed his shot glass down on the bar. 'I'll fucking kill him, I'll fucking kill both of them,' he said to me. I had a mind to take him up on it, you know?"

Fretz exhaled and smiled and shook his head. "How did we get on this?" he said.

There was an uncomfortable silence. It occurred to me again that this was the first time I had ever really done anything with him, outside of just chatting in bars.

"I asked you how you got into blowing up things."

"Oh yeah, how I started shooting heads," he said, grinning a little bit. He had put the strap on and he let the gun hang freely around his neck. He rubbed the back of his head. "So I had a few drinks and then called the house. She didn't answer. She let the answering machine come on. 'Hey, honey, just checking in,' I said into the machine. 'We're up here in Williamsport almost at the cabin. Hope you're having a good time there at home. Hope you're having a good time doing your *things around the house*.' I had to say that to her, *your things around the house*, Jesus fucking Christ," he said.

Fretz seemed aware that his sentences were gaining speed and he paused for a couple of seconds and stared in at the corral next to the barn where the man had been training the horse. I was unsure if he was through talking, but I decided I should express my condolences for the whole affair anyway.

"Fretz, I'm sorry about all that . . ."

"So I did another shot and said goodbye to the drunk at the bar and drove over to the house. I turned out the lights as I eased up and I parked a few houses down the street. I didn't want them to see me out front."

He jammed his hand on the bottom of the clip to make sure it was in tight.

"I just sat there in the car for an hour waiting for them to come out, but they were in for the night. They were in for the night to fuck, you know?"

He stared at me again, but I didn't know what to say so I just stared back at him. He took the gun in both hands and pointed it at the Tide bottle hanging from the jungle gym.

"So I went in through the basement door . . ." He held the trigger down on the gun. *Rat-a-tat-tat-tat-tat-tat.* The Tide bottle swung maniacally. ". . . and I came up through the kitchen . . ." *Rat-a-tat-tat-tat-tat.* Two of the tennis ball cans flew up in the air. ". . . where I knew . . ." *Rat-a-tat.* ". . . they wouldn't hear me." *Rat-a-tat-tat-tat.* He held the gun loosely in one hand as he walked over and picked up one of the heads by the hair. He swung it back and forth, underhand, and he hurled it up in the air. *Rat-a-tat-tat-tat-tat-tat. Tat-tat-tat-tat.* He hit it a few times as it flew, and followed it with the barrel of the gun as it landed on the ground. "And then . . ." *Rat-a-tat-tat-tat.* The head gyrated and wobbled, changing the direction it was rolling each time it was hit. Pieces of rubber and hair splattered and flew. ". . . I took the gun out of the living room dresser drawer."

"The gun?" I said.

He stopped and looked at me.

"Yeah, we kept a gun around."

"I thought you said you hated guns."

"I did. I didn't want it there. It was part of her fear thing. She insisted on having it, that's what I've been telling you," he said.

He picked up the other head and drop-kicked it toward the dirt pile. *Rat-a-tat-tat-tat.* He aimed from the hip this time and his shots were less accurate. Dirt flew up all around it, and the head came to rest near the other one.

"I walked in on them in the bedroom." He sprayed machine-gun fire back and forth over the heads. "They were buck naked." *Rat-a-tat-tat-tat-tat-tat.* "Buck fucking naked." *Rat-a-tat-tat-tat-tat-tat.*

" 'You've got a lot of fucking nerve marching in like this,' the guy said. 'You've got a lot of fucking nerve fucking my wife,' I told him."

Fretz paused again and looked at me. I felt obligated to speak.

"Jesus," I said.

"Fucking Jesus Christ is right," he said.

"What did you do?"

"What do you think I did?"

"You didn't shoot them, obviously."

"No, I didn't shoot them," he said.

"But you could have."

"Damn right I could have. And plenty of better men would have," he said. "I was standing over my wife and one of our friends with both of them buck naked in bed and I didn't blow them away," he said.

He stared at me as if he expected me to respond again, but I wasn't sure I understood. It was supposed to be this wonderful thing that he didn't blow their brains out. And in some bizarre way, it was supposed to explain his infatuation with blowing up rubber heads.

"Can you believe that nonsense?" he said.

I just peered back at him, hoping he would look away or start shooting again, but he didn't. He stared at me, and when I didn't say anything he undid the strap from the machine gun and walked over and leaned against the hood of his beat-up car. He shook his head, stared off at the cornfields, and sighed.

"These Amish are good people. Hardworking, peace-loving, family people," he said.

I looked in at the house and then out at the fields.

"They farm *all* of this," he said.

We stood in uncomfortable silence for a while, both of us staring off at the corn. I saw him rub his eye and then he looked up at me again. His face was contorted in a way I hadn't seen on him before. His eyes were squinched up and his lips were pursed together like an old man without teeth. His head was set down in his neck in a way that exaggerated his double chin.

"There are only a few good people left in this world," he said.

It was odd what I thought of then. It was the way Fretz's head was receded into his shoulders, shortening his neck, I think, that made me remember a giant sea turtle I had seen once on an island in the Caribbean. It was a loggerhead, the kind that lives to be over a hundred years old. Some Bahamians had kept it alive for a few days, kept it tied by the leg to a mangrove tree. I happened to be there the evening they slaughtered it. When they rolled it over on its back and cut the nylon rope around its leg, it started flapping its fins or legs or whatever it is that they have. There was something human about it—about its struggle—the way the huge turtle slapped its fins like hands on its chest and the way its head, practically the size of a basketball, receded tentatively and knowingly into its shell. I remember staring at the wrinkled-up flesh around its neck and at its squinting eyes just before they slit its throat and ran the tip of the knife along the soft flesh of its underside.

"Only a few good people," he said again. He was staring at me. I realized my mind had drifted.

"Only a few good people," I said.

"Well . . ." He looked over at the Amish farmhouse and then back at the heads on the ground under the homemade jungle gym. One of them had its face down, away from us, but the other was facing us. It was lying on its side with one of its cheeks pressed against the ground, and it appeared to be looking at me. "You want to try this beast?" he said.

I stared at the head staring at me and then I looked up at Fretz again. He looked terrified to me, like everything was riding on the answer I gave him.

"Sure, I'll fire a round or two," I said.

His face relaxed, and he stood up straight and smiled and stretched his neck upward so his double chin disappeared.

"Good, it'll probably be good for you," he said.

Diet

Regularly, my father told my mother she was fat. If one of us didn't take a piece of fish when the plate was passed, my father's spoon would crack like a hammer on our heads. The diet was for my mother mostly, but for all of us, he said. Once when the spoon fell on me, the youngest son, my mother tried to intervene, but he dragged her from the table by her hair.

Beauty Queen

My ex-wife was a beauty queen.

Her first crown came at age thirteen. The Dairy Princess. I saw
the picture shortly after we started dating. It was a Polaroid. She
was standing on a parade float, waving to the Reading, Pennsylvania, hometown crowd with that fake but convincing smile that
came so naturally for her. There were live Holstein cows with
swollen, milk-filled udders chained up on both sides of her.

Her prize for that contest was a $25 savings bond and the right
to keep the skimpy dress they made her wear for the parade. She
had no breasts at that age, but the Dairy Princess judges were
intent on having her show what little she had. A subliminal *milk*
thing, I suppose. The dress was a halter top that exposed what
would have been her cleavage if she had been old enough. It
sucked in at her tiny waist so it fit snug around her hips and then it
fluffed out again below her ass. It was hemmed a good two or three

inches above her knees to expose plenty of leg. It was white for purity, virginity, and dairy products.

There was a gaudy, glass-jewel crown, too, but she didn't get the honor of keeping it. (Apparently that was too valuable to replace from year to year.) It was hard to see in the picture, but Melody—even her name was perfect for pageants—remembered it in perfect detail. It had white and blue stones all around the outside with a glass Holstein cow in the front as a kind of centerpiece. There was a cluster of pink cubic zirconia stones for an udder and—this was the unbelievable thing—tiny red stones for nipples. "You can almost see the little teets," I remember her saying the first time she showed me the picture.

I don't think she ever lost the sort of juvenile beauty she had in that Dairy Princess Polaroid. Even in adulthood, she had the same long, slender, delicious arms. And her breasts never really grew that large. They were shapely, mind you, above her stomach, which was always amazingly flat, and they were a fine accent to her small, tight, suitably ovular buttocks, but they weren't huge in the conventional sense. Her legs were long and thin and perfect. That's what she was, after all, *perfect*. She wasn't the quintessential voluptuous measurements. She was long and lean. Long and lean and angular. Even her gorgeous face was angular. High cheekbones, thin lips, a sharp, aggressive grin . . .

There was a series of other achievements, too. At age sixteen she became the Poultry Queen. That one was very similar to the dairy contest: a skimpy dress, a crown, a parade, live animals. There was a little talent part to it, too—a superficial effort to legitimize the whole affair. It was a slightly bigger deal, I suppose. The contestants were older—*late* adolescence—so there was also a swimsuit part to the judging. The only other difference was that there were chickens chained next to her on the parade float—chickens instead of Holstein cows.

Some of her honors were less overt. They were social honors instead of actual contests. When she was in eighth grade, the captain of the varsity soccer team asked her out on a date, and in ninth grade the hunky quarterback of the football team courted her. The hard thing about those situations for her girlfriends, she told me, was that the guys were more than just athletic and handsome, they were smart, even stylish. There were junior and senior girls who wanted to scratch her eyes out just because the boys were attracted to her. It wasn't Melody's fault. She couldn't help that she was beautiful.

Things like that went on happening, again not because she ran over people, but because things just came to her. In her junior year, she was voted Homecoming Queen as a write-in on the ballot. It wasn't supposed to be allowed, but after she won she went in and discussed the matter with the balding, potbellied principal— "flirted with him a *tad*," she admitted—and he decided to make an exception because of "her diligence in her studies" and "her pleasant, positive attitude." She was a "model student" and he was "thrilled" to have her represent Ridgemont at the homecoming parade. *"Model. Thrilled,"* she said, rolling her eyes and shaking her head the first time she told me that story.

On top of all this, Melody was an exceptional athlete. And the truly amazing thing was, even that came easily for her. I remember after one of her college track meets she said to me, "All I have to do is run fast like when I played kick the can or prisoner's base as a kid." It didn't require meticulous training or mental effort for her like it did for, say, me in tennis. It always intrigued me: the same long, slender legs that won her beauty contests won her state medals in the fifty- and one-hundred-yard dashes. She could pump her legs like pistons and she still looked like she was gliding when she ran.

Watching her run, in fact, is how I fell in love with her. I played on the college tennis team and the courts were up on the hill next to the track. After my grueling, disciplined workouts I would walk down and sit on the hill and watch her work out with the team. It looked almost as if she was floating when she ran, *gliding* or *floating,* yet moving along the surface of the land. Sometimes I would carry my racquets all the way to the bottom of the hill, right next to the track, and watch her up close where I could study the muscles in her calves and the backs of her thighs. After each sprint she would walk slowly back to the starting line, her muscles flexing and bulging wonderfully with each step. Her calves especially—they'd bounce into a taut, flexed position as she pushed off with the ball of her foot. You could see that they were hard, but they *bounced,* almost like fat, even though they definitely weren't fat. No, they certainly weren't fat. They were tight, *pure muscle.* That was obvious enough.

When she walked between sprints, she'd swing her arms at her sides in a kind of a swagger. She would slump her shoulders and walk leaning back, a little duck-footed, breathing heavily, with her mouth open. It didn't matter that she walked with poor posture, it only made her sexier somehow. It only meant that she was that comfortable with her body. I'd stare and imagine the heat of her blood pumping. Her high cheekbones, her firm jaw, and the sweat on her upper lip . . . they all gave her beauty a delicate masculinity. She looked so alive and so confident. Jesus, she was ravishing.

Things didn't come as easily for me as they did for her, and in a certain sense I found it strange, her attraction to me. I worked very hard at the things I did. My tennis, for instance, wasn't anything like running for Melody. I played because it was the kind of sport in which I could make up for my mediocre athletic ability with grit. I could spend hundreds of hours practicing the ball toss for the serve until I got it just right. I could hit thousands of backhands trying to perfect my shoulder turn and my weight transfer. I could use my mind to beat guys who, frankly, had the kind of natural athletic ability that Melody had. If I played a big serve-and-volleyer, I'd frustrate him by hitting soft slices at his feet and then lobbing over him. If I played a big-hitting baseliner, I'd bait him into going for too much by hitting high, loopy balls without a lot of pace, deep into the court.

I was in decent shape, but I wasn't nearly as good looking as she was, that's for certain. My nose was too big—it still is—and I was kind of gangly, almost skinny. I had had pretty bad acne in high school and I was still on the tail end of that. I definitely wasn't one of the hunky quarterbacks or soccer stars she was used to dating.

But school did come fairly easily for me, and looking back on everything, I'm certain that must have had something to do with why she was attracted to me. I wasn't an exceptional student, don't get me wrong, but I could converse about a lot of things and sound, to her at least, as if I knew what I was talking about. I could make her laugh, too. That must have been a big part of it. I didn't see it then, but I realize now that she saw me as a kind of a bridge between her body and her mind. A way for her to grow, a way for her to pass from the physical to the cerebral. All her life she had been affirmed for her body. Even when she was a child— the dresses she got as presents, the adolescent beauty contests, people pinching her cheeks and raving about what a cutie she was. I came along at a time when she was trying to break out of all that.

It wasn't that I was that smart or that athletic, but that's just it, it was the combination. I was the bridge, the liaison, the mind-to-body guru.

I remember the first time we chatted in the library.

"Do you believe that stuff?" I said.

She was studying a developmental psychology text and I went down on one knee next to her table. Her face flushed and then she recomposed.

"Well, it is my major," she said.

"Psych?"

"Yes, *psychology*," she said.

I should have been put off, but I was willing to risk my personal dignity.

"I've been doing sociology," I said.

"*Doing* it?" she said, raising her eyebrows.

"I'm thinking about majoring," I said.

There was an awkward pause and then she said, "Did you want something?"

I wanted to say, *"Yes, you,"* but I was just smart enough at that age to refrain from that kind of thing. I didn't really have a good reason for approaching her except that I was attracted to her physically. I thought on my feet. She was in one of my classes.

"Do you have the Western Civ assignment for tomorrow?" I said.

She reached in her purse and pulled out a thin black book that said *Academic Planner* across the top. That impressed me because I never organized my own studying. She opened it and pointed to the name of the text and the page numbers which she had neatly written in the square for that day.

"Thanks. Thank you very much," I said, leaving.

. . .

But I wasn't going to give up that easily. Ours was a small college and there were opportunities for me to pontificate, if not directly to her, at least in her presence. My last name was Hues and hers was Henderson so we ended up in the same weekly discussion group for our Western Civilization class. One day in one of those discussions I made what was really a fairly unimpressive, unoriginal comment about how I didn't think it was right that we studied the Greeks—as if they were right about everything—and ignored the Eastern cultural arts and philosophies.

"What does everyone think about Will's comment?" the graduate student discussion leader said.

Maybe it sounded profound for a college freshman, I don't know. In any case, it impressed Melody. I saw her forehead wrinkle up and I saw her put her hand on her chin. I caught her staring at me two or three more times before the end of class. That was all I needed (God knows you don't need much at that age). That night I went looking for her in the library.

"What did you think of the discussion today?" I said, going down on one knee again.

She closed her psychology text and slid it to the upper right corner of the study carrel.

"It was interesting," she said.

"Psych again?" I said, pointing to the textbook she had closed.

Her forehead wrinkled up like it had in class.

"So did you *think* of that . . . comment . . . or did you *read* it?"

"Oh . . . in class?" I could feel the sweat cranking up in my armpits. "Some of both, I guess," I said.

I went on and bullshitted about something we had covered in Intro to Sociology. Basic nature/nurture questions. I argued for nurture, which impressed her. She had been lapping up the stuff in her psychology courses uncritically.

"Take the case of children, female children, being given dollies to play with while boys are given balls, tractors, or toy guns. Little girls are *taught* to be soft. They're taught to like dollies, while boys are taught to play with tractors and guns."

Again, not especially novel ideas, but they impressed her. She nodded and smiled. She thought it was cute that I called them "dollies."

"Psychologists tend to assume the innateness of girls' affinity for dolls. Sociologists, on the other hand, ask questions like, 'Who taught them to like dollies? What are the large-scale social consequences of teaching boys to be competitive or rugged while teaching girls to look pretty, to *nurture* things?' "

She nodded and rubbed her forehead again.

"I mean, are you all sugar and spice?"

She smiled and her lower jaw came out like it did when she was walking up the track after a sprint. "Hardly," she said.

"And I'm not all snakes and snails," I said, smiling at her. "Like, what are we saying to little girls when we give them Barbies?"

The corner of her mouth twitched and she slouched in her chair. It made me think of her sexy, poor-postured, post-sprint swagger. She put her hands behind her head and looked straight into mine with her fabulous green eyes.

"This is more interesting than my reading," she said. "Do you want to get some pancakes?"

My college tennis coach—*Coach* Phooder, he insisted we call him—complained about things like skim milk, "fags," and vegetarians. He drank soda constantly, ate lots of candy bars, and ate multiple plates of fried French toast sticks at the Shoney's brunch bar where he took us for pregame meals.

The afternoon after his wife gave birth to their third child, he showed up late for tennis practice. We had already scattered out on the courts and started playing, but he called us in, gathered us around, and told us to congratulate him. "My wife just had my third child. A boy this time, *finally*," he said. He had been up all night, and after the successful delivery, he had gone to Harry's Diner and eaten their *Mother Load.* He smiled when he said *Mother Load* and then he told us what the dish consisted of—ham, eggs, bacon, sausage, scrapple, and pancakes. He looked at his fingernails which, I remember thinking, probably still had amniotic fluid underneath them. "I got the eggs sunny-side, extra-runny," he said. The team smiled and laughed. I did, too, probably. But then he said something I'll never forget. He got a very serious look on his face. His pudgy cheeks sucked in, he pursed his lips, and his head receded into his shoulders, adding another roll to his already multiple chins.

"You know," he said, looking pensively off over our heads, "they had to do a cesarean section in the end." I thought he was going to say something tender, something about how helping his wife deliver their child had affected him. He shook his head like he was in pain. "So I gave the doctor a twenty, told him to sew her up a little tighter for me."

When I met Melody I wasn't a virgin. Unfortunately for both of us, that wasn't the case with her.

I had had sex myself with only one person, the summer before. For some reason I hadn't done it with anyone in high school which, I think, was unusual for someone my age. I'd had a couple of girlfriends, and I had fooled around a little, but for a number of reasons, I hadn't wanted to sleep with them. For one, there was a lot going on at home. My father had been cheating on my mother for years. My two older brothers were angry adolescents—angry at the adult world, which, they thought, was comprised of all *hypocrites*. They did drugs, listened to Kiss, and treated my mother violently (so had my father before my parents separated). My brothers also, as a kind of further symbol of their defiance, had sex with their girlfriends in my mother's basement. But my mother was very good to me and I sided with her on almost everything. It seemed—my brothers' basement sex—almost like an actual part of their violence toward her. I heard them often and it disgusted me.

My father moved out when I was twelve, but there was one instance before he left, but after all of us knew he was cheating on her, when I walked in on my parents having sex. He was on top of her, pumping away. Maybe it would have felt okay in a different context, but he was already cheating on her and there she was letting him fuck her. And, of course, he had been beating up on her for years, so why hadn't she stopped screwing him years before? That's what it was to me, *fucking* and *screwing*. It wasn't *making love*, that's for certain.

In junior high, my summer Bible camp counselor had told us that sex out of wedlock was sinful and that if you did it, you would reap what you sowed. I was groping for things to believe in around that time, and given what was going on at home, it sounded convincing to me. The camp preacher talked about *saving yourself* for your mate and for a while I thought I would do it. But when I began to realize how much of what I learned at summer Bible camp was ridiculous—like that the world was four thousand years old—I rethought the sex issue. At some point, I decided I just wanted to see what the big deal was. I had sex with Marianne Connely in her parents' bed one weekend when they were away. Marianne had done it before and she made me feel very comfortable even though I didn't know what I was doing. Probably partly because we were doing it for, among others, the simple reason that we liked each other, I was pleasantly surprised to discover that I didn't feel dirty afterwards. It wasn't the big deal that the camp preacher had said it would be. My penis didn't fall off. We both enjoyed it. We did it eight times in three days.

Still, I had waited a long time to have sex—much longer than most guys my age—and I was very sensitive to the idea of someone being cautious or afraid. I could empathize with someone idealizing it. I could respect someone *saving themselves* or thinking they were protecting themselves emotionally by choosing to wait until they found the right one.

It didn't add up at first, Mel's being a virgin. Of all people, you'd think that a beauty queen would, with all the pressure and opportunities, lose her virginity before college. If I'd have guessed on our first or second date, I'd have said she'd had sex at age fourteen in the back of one of her high school quarterback boyfriend's Chevrolets. But that wasn't Mel. She wasn't unaffectionate or prudish, not at all, she just took her body—its beauty, health, and sanctity—very seriously. She wasn't unsexual, not by any means. She masturbated daily, and she talked openly to me about her desire for pleasure. She would take my hand and show me where to touch her, even use it to touch herself. She'd have multiple orgasms, three or four in a session. She'd go down on me and she had, I found out later, done the same for her high school boyfriends. She'd just never had intercourse.

You must understand that I tried very hard to be very sensitive to her physically. I never pushed her. I waited for *her* to give *me* the signal.

On the way home from one of our away matches, Coach Phooder liked to think of little games for the team to play. This one came to him while he and Luis Lopez were going through the names of the women on the field hockey team, asking everyone "would you," and then counting yes or no votes. Phooder presented the idea for the new game in the same way he told the joke about sewing up his wife after she had had their baby. He quieted the van and got everyone's undivided attention.

"Okay, guys, I want you guys to come to a consensus." He spoke in the same deep, authoritative voice he used when he told us to run sprints. "The *five most fuckable*." You could tell he was very pleased with himself. It was a breakthrough idea for him. Sudden illumination. "Give me the list when you're through," he said.

In the early stages of the exercise, there was considerable discussion about whether *fuckability* could also involve personality and intelligence. I had been trying to ignore everything, pretending to listen to my Walkman, but I couldn't help myself. I slipped off my headphones and said something that I thought, at the time, was a kind of courageous championing of women's issues.

"It should involve more than just looks," I said.

It was the first time that I was participating actively in any of their *would you, fuckability* games, and it felt in that moment as if everyone was scrutinizing me. The van went quiet except for the hum of the tires on the highway, and everyone turned around and stared at me.

Coach Phooder broke the silence.

"Looks. This is just looks," he called from the driver's seat.

I don't think he intended it as a joke, but everyone laughed. His voice was deep and commanding again and it set the tone for the debates in the next twenty minutes. The *just looks* dictum seemed to amplify the degree to which women were discussed like pieces of meat. There were extensive arguments over the shape of hips, size of breasts, tightness and contour of asses. Luis Lopez offered, in numerous cases, what he claimed was experiential knowledge.

"I'll bet she smells," Nathan Georgalis said of Amy Cornelius.

"Oh, she does, let me tell you," Luis Lopez announced, raising his eyebrows.

The group was working toward a consensus for each ranking like Coach Phooder had insisted, but often when it seemed that one of the spots was just about to be set, a dissenter would protest and put the issue back on the floor.

"Her ass is too big," Mark Wellesley said of Melissa Lichty.

"Ah, Melissa Lick-me," Bobby Witmer added, slouching in his seat and spreading his legs.

When the discussion started to stray into directionless banter and argument, Luis Lopez brought it into focus again.

"Look, it's only the four spot we're talking about," he said.

"No fuck, give it to Lick-me," Bobby chimed.

"All right, guys, Melissa Lick-me's spot for the four spot." He pounded a tennis racquet like a mallet on the seat in front of him. "All in favor? All opposed?" He counted the hands. "Miss Lick-me it is. Her spot takes the four spot," he said, pounding his racquet again.

There had been a brainstorm at the beginning, a calling out of women who were in the pool, and Melody's name had received the most emphatic moans and hoots. The five and four positions were filled and Charity Newhouse was about to fill the third ranking. I felt a constriction in my throat, like my esophagus was narrowing. The thought of them violating her verbally infuriated me. I didn't want to hear Luis Lopez say something about Mel's *snatch,* and I was afraid I'd explode if Coach Phooder said anything vulgar about her at all. The last thing I wanted was a sexual image of Phooder and Melody in my head. I was also fearing my own humiliation. I knew that everyone knew I was dating Melody. I was afraid they'd put me on the spot somehow, force me to either participate or defend her, insist that I talk about our sexual relationship.

Charity Newhouse, or *Free Charity,* as Bobby Witmer called her, was declared the third position. That left Rebecca Slaybaugh and Melody.

"Rebecca Slaybaugh, number two," Nathan Georgalis announced.

"Más despacio," Luis Lopez said. "How about some discussion? I mean, this is the *number one most fuckable* we're talking about. Let's put it back on the floor. Pros and cons? Becky Slay-all or Melody Henderson?"

"Slaybaugh has the tits for it," Georgalis said.

Coach Phooder smiled and shook his head. "Oh, yes, she is *filthy,*" he said, which meant she was attractive, apparently.

"Oh, she's a *tramp,*" Ricky Richards said.

"A fucking whore," Lopez said, sighing. "Fuckablicious," he said. He looked upset with desire, almost disturbed.

"Rebecca Slay-all," Witmer said.

"If tits could kill," Georgalis added, pleased with the course of things.

Luis liked to see everyone participate in the discussion, so he invited Jeremy Johnson, who had been nearly as silent as me, to speak. "And what about you, Mr. Johnson? Every man has an opinion on pussy."

"I yield to the gentleman from Oregon. Rebecca Slay-all is my vote," Jeremy said.

It seemed like everyone was about to settle on her for number one, even Luis Lopez, and then Coach Phooder interfered.

"Wait a minute. Slaybaugh *is* a little chunky, *isn't* she?" he said.

I glared at Phooder, thinking about how fat he was himself. Every other week he talked about going on some kind of diet, but he never did it. He took a bite of a Milky Way he had just opened and washed it down with a swig of Mountain Dew.

"I mean, I know you guys are young and all, but it's not *all about tits.*"

There was an awkward silence while everyone considered Phooder's comments carefully, and then Luis Lopez, sensing the group's need for leadership, took charge again.

"He's right, Coach is right," Luis said. "We need to consider this carefully. Let's talk about Mel Henderson's ass. *Bonito ass. Culito bonito,*" he said.

Luis was fluent in Spanish, and while I'm not sure that it worked, he liked to try to use his Spanish and his knowledge of wine—his grandparents owned a small winery in Chile—to charm women. The *Latino Love Machine,* he had dubbed himself one day in practice, partly joking, but mostly serious. When attractive women walked by the courts, he made a kind of a hissing sound. He made that sound at this moment.

"*Tssss, tsssss.* Mell-o-deee Heeend-eer-son, *fucky fucky,*" he said, exaggerating his Spanish accent.

Everyone laughed except Nathan Georgalis. He was pretending to be genuinely hurt by the suggestion that he was overemphasizing Rebecca Slaybaugh's chest.

"You need something to grab on to," he protested.

"*Bueno,* but they don't have to be tits," Luis said.

"Look, Mel Henderson has no chest. *Nothing*," he said. "I mean, what will the baby eat? You can't carry milk in those things."

I thought about Mel in the low-cut, white Dairy Princess dress.

"Who said anything about kids?" Luis said.

I saw Coach Phooder reach up and adjust the mirror so he could see me again. He tilted back his head to get the proper angle and said, "Why don't you guys ask Hues? He's been fucking her, hasn't he?" he said.

I was in the seat in the very back of the van. Everyone turned around and peered at me.

"That true, Hues?" Luis said. He was smiling. Everyone was, actually. "She let you fuck her yet?" he said.

I tried to think of something to say, but I couldn't, I just stared back at them. I could feel my face flushing.

"I bet she's a screamer," Coach Phooder said.

I felt a surge of angry energy move up the back of my neck and out into my arms.

"I bet she bled the first time you fucked her. I'll bet *I* could make her bleed," Phooder said.

I wanted to shout an insult at him, something random and unrelated, like how ugly and disgusting the mole on his nose was, or how many bags of potato chips he averaged during *Monday Night Football.* I wanted to punch him in the mouth and watch his fat face bleed.

"How about it, Hues? What's your vote?" Luis said. "Tits or ass? Slaybaugh's bouncing balls or *culito bonito,* your skank's tight little ass?"

I looked up at Coach Phooder in the front of the van and caught a glimpse of his round face in the rearview. He was gnawing on his Milky Way again.

"Ass," I said. I kept watching Phooder in the mirror. He put his candy bar down, smirked, and took another sip of his soda. "My vote is ass. For Melody," I said.

That night when we got back from the tennis match there was a note from Mel on my dorm room door. It said, *"Waiting for you. Roommate gone for the weekend."* I showered and dressed in the pair of old jeans that I knew she liked on me. Even though I usually wore T-shirts, I put on a nice, soft, long-sleeved, collared oxford that I thought she'd appreciate.

When I got to her dorm room and knocked, she said calmly, seductively, "It's open, come in."

She was under the covers with her shirt off. She didn't even sit up in bed when I entered. There was a candle burning on her desk—no other light in the room. It was making shadows on the wall opposite the bed. She hadn't been sleeping, it was clear, but she didn't sit up to greet me. She just rolled over on her side in a sort of fetal position, with her elbows in front of her breasts and her hands curled up on the pillow, under her chin.

"I've been waiting for you," she said.

I realized how typically masculine it was to be attracted to her *softness,* but I couldn't help myself. She looked so soft and beautiful to me at that moment. She loved soft, silky things, and the comforter she was cuddled up in was down, cream-colored, and the highest thread count available. It looked so good over her breasts, against the milky, pale skin on her shoulders and neck. Randomly, I pictured Luis Lopez looking at me, saying, "Tits or ass?" It made me suddenly furious, but there was nothing I could do about it, it was just there in my head. I tried to block it out and lay down next to her with my shoes and clothes on. I touched her cheek with my fingertips.

"You look beautiful," I said.

She just stared at my eyes blankly and I was afraid for a moment I had said something wrong, that I should have said something about *who she was* instead of how she looked. I felt another surge of anger at Coach Phooder and Luis Lopez and I decided it was their fault that her physical beauty was the first thing on my tongue.

"Did you miss me?" she said.

"I was thinking about you the whole trip."

"Me too," she said.

She touched my face with her gentle hand and she lifted up my shirt and touched her fingertips to my belly. She ran her hand up onto my chest and neck and then back down my hip. It felt tingly, shivery, wonderful.

"Do you like that?"

"I do," I said.

"Take your pants off," she said.

I kicked my shoes off and they fell, one at a time, with intrusive thuds, onto the floor. They were loud, obnoxious sounds and they made me feel like we weren't alone, as if people were eavesdropping on us.

"Your roommate's gone?"

"Long gone," she said.

"Should I lock the door?"

"If it makes you more comfortable," she said.

I got up and locked it and then, with my back turned, took my pants off. I was wearing a pair of boxer shorts that she had bought for me. I left those on and took my long-sleeved shirt off. I left on my white undershirt and crawled in next to her, under the comforter. She cupped both hands on my cheeks and stared at me so intensely that it looked almost as if she was angry. She kissed me and I felt her hips pressing into mine.

"Oh, God," I said.

"What?" she said.

She held the back of my head with one hand as she kissed my neck and chest.

"You," I said, arching my back.

"Is there something wrong?"

"No, nothing's wrong," I said.

Then she said, somewhat suddenly, "Wilson, will you touch me?" It wasn't unusual for her to ask me like that, but it surprised me this time for some reason—I think because I was still thinking about the van conversation. I tried as hard as I could not to, but I couldn't help but think of her request in these terms: that I was in bed with the *number one most fuckable* and that she was asking me to *touch* her.

She rolled onto her back and I reached down between her legs. She was naked. I was going to lick my fingers, but she was already lubricated. It only took three or four minutes for her to climax, and after she came once, she held my hand there so I'd keep touching her. In the next five minutes, with me just touching her, she had two smaller orgasms. After the last one, she put both her hands on my cheeks and stared at me. Her eyes were moist and she gazed at me with her mouth slightly open.

"Sometimes I wonder what it's like to feel you," she said.

My hand was still between her legs.

"To feel me?"

"To feel you *inside* of me."

I thought I understood, but I wasn't sure.

"You mean my fingers?"

"No, *you,* Wilson."

I put my arms around her and snuggled my face up under her chin.

"I mean *you, inside* of me."

I caressed her face and hair and I rested my head on her chest. I sighed. I felt both wonderful and miserable.

"Don't you want to?" she asked.

If I was going to say something, this was the time. This was the time for me to tell her I wasn't a virgin.

"I do want to," I said.

"Are you scared?"

"A little, I guess."

She rubbed my head maternally. "Ah, of course you are," she said.

We didn't have sex then, but looking back on it now, I think it was that moment that I value as much as any in our entire relationship. I just lay there with my head on her breasts. I could feel her chest rise and fall underneath my head and I could hear her heart beating. I felt the vibration of both thumps as it pumped blood in the one side of her heart and out the other. I thought about the blood gurgling through her arteries, racing out her veins, into her capillaries, and then spreading out into her cells. It felt so pure between us. We weren't having sex, but it was still as if our bodies were actually sharing fluid, sharing blood, passing oxygen and nourishment back and forth to each other. It was as if the blood her heart was pumping, the oxygen contained in it, spread out through her capillaries to the surface of her skin and jumped over onto mine, into me. It felt as though nothing I could say could taint our closeness. But of course that feeling—the feeling that nothing can come between you and another human being—is a deceit, and now I realize that's what it is. It's like a lie you tell yourself. It's like believing in God because of your need to believe, instead of because God actually exists.

"Wilson, can I ask you a question?" she said.

"Sure," I told her.

"You've never had sex before, have you?" she asked.

The way she phrased the question, it seemed like I had no choice but to give the right answer, the answer she wanted. It came out before I knew what had happened.

"No," I said, ridiculously.

I panicked, started plotting how I was going to explain my spontaneous lie, my "no" answer. I planned to tell her the truth, later.

"Are you sure nothing's wrong?" she said.

"Yes, I'm sure," I said.

This was exactly one week after she told me she wanted to sleep with me. It was a Friday again. We didn't have a tennis match on this weekend, which was unusual, and it was probably partly for the reason that Coach Phooder was bored that he had to drum up something different for us to do in practice.

There was room for one tennis court in the school gymnasium and occasionally, when it rained, we went inside and practiced on it. There was a temporary indoor net we set up. The court wasn't ideal because the surface was very fast, much faster than the normal hard courts we played all of our matches on. For that reason the indoor practices were usually informal. If it rained and we had to go into the gym, we'd just practice our serves or do something casual. But this was beyond casual.

"We're going inside," Phooder announced, halfway through our outdoor practice.

It wasn't raining and no one could figure out why we were going in, but Phooder wasn't the kind of coach who appreciated questions or criticism. Nobody protested.

When we got in, he told us to set up the net. Luis and I did it without asking questions. He said, "Georgalis and Witmer, shut all the doors. Make sure they're latched, and *locked.*" There was an echo in the gym and Phooder's deep, military like voice resounded. The bleachers were all stacked up to the wall. It hadn't rained in a number of weeks so no one had been in to use the gym. The floor was all dusty.

When all of the doors were locked, he called us to the net and said, "Guys, we're going to work on pressure tennis today. *Pressure tennis.*" He smirked and swung his arms behind his back like he was stretching them. His chest and belly protruded. "Postseason is coming up. We can't have anybody choking."

It was tense and quiet. Outside, the sun was shining.

"Today we'll be playing *strip tennis,*" he said.

Everybody smiled and laughed nervously, as if he was joking, but he wasn't joking. Not at all. He was serious.

"Whoever ends up naked first runs a suicide . . . with everybody watching. One article of clothing per lost point," he said.

If he had been *completely* authoritative, he couldn't have pulled it off, but he said it with a little smirk on his face—in the same way he had ordered the *"five most fuckable"* game. Phooder commanded authority, but he could also successfully work this *one-of-the-guys* attitude. That can be dangerous for a coach. I've been on teams where that collapsed into a situation in which the players could look right at the coach and say, "Fuck off, Coach, we're not doing sprints today," but Phooder combined his chummy attitude with an excessively masculine, confident air. He was able to get us to do things most coaches couldn't have.

"Let's go, four on a side. Line it up," he said.

There was some giggling and grumbling as we divided up on opposite sides of the court, but everybody was doing it.

"*Ay, Dios mío,*" Luis Lopez mumbled as we set up on the baseline. "Fucking coach is *loco,*" he said, smiling.

Actually, almost everyone was smiling, only because they didn't know what else to do. There was no way to protest. If you did, you set yourself up for major abuse. I could just hear it. Why didn't you want to play? What was the big deal? Were you ashamed of your body? Were you a *fag* or something?

The way it worked was, Phooder fed a ball to one of the players to start the point. The thing about that was that if it was an easy feed, the player he hit the first ball to could gain an advantage right away before the rally even began. Sometimes, depending on who was up, he'd make the feed so easy they could approach the net on the first shot. It wasn't fair. Phooder was affecting the outcome. And starting the point with a groundstroke instead of a serve hurt me. My serve was the best part of my game. Phooder knew that.

Every time you lost a point you had to take off an article of clothing. Even that rule left some with an unfair advantage. Some guys happened to have worn a lot of accessories, like wristbands, hats, and headbands, but I didn't wear all that stuff. I just had my shorts, a T-shirt, my shoes, and my socks. Also, Phooder invented some of the rules as we played and in that way he influenced who had to get naked. He let some guys count things you wouldn't normally think of as clothes, things like watches and necklaces. He even let Bobby Witmer count his ankle wrap. He actually let him take off individual strips of tape and count each strip as a piece of clothing.

I'm certain that Phooder wanted to see me humiliated. He could sense my discomfort with his adolescent jokes, his *fuckability* games, and he saw it as a threat to his authority. It was as if he knew the game would take me apart, that I'd be more likely to collapse mentally than anyone else on the team. He wanted to see me squirm, among other things.

I was one of the best players, the number two seed, and I was usually very strong mentally, but in this situation I tightened up horribly. It's a term in tennis, *tightening up*. Your muscles need to be loose and limber to hit the ball with any power or accuracy. It's not like football or some sport where you can just flex your muscles and grit your teeth and have it help you. It's about levers and fluidity. You actually have to relax physically. That mental aspect was actually what attracted me to tennis, but in *strip tennis* my mental game collapsed. It was like I knew before we even started that I'd lose. I remembered how I ended up feeling naked at the end of all the sex jokes, so I thought I'd probably be the one to get screwed and run the suicide with no clothes on. I kept thinking, "I'm going to choke, I'm going to lose."

Everyone got into it. What else was there to do? They all hooted and hollered and laughed while the points were being played. If someone hit a great shot with half their clothes off, it was a much greater accomplishment even than hitting a winner in a real collegiate match. This was real pressure.

Luis Lopez and I were the first ones to get down to just our underwear. He had come to practice without a shirt, which he often did so that he could show off his chest to the women on the way to the courts. On this day, it had backfired on him.

"Okay, crunch time," Phooder said. He looked very pleased. He usually tried to play it cool when he told a joke himself or when he thought something was funny, but he was grinning like I never saw him grin. "The *Latin Love Machine* versus . . ." He paused and scratched his chin while he thought of a nickname for me. "The *Latin Love Machine* versus . . . *the Nuke*," he said.

I don't know quite what he meant by it, but it wasn't a compliment. I was skinny back then and, as I said, my nose was a little too large. My hair was frizzy and big.

"*Mi Dios*, el *Nuke*," Luis said, buckling over.

The whole team started trying it out, saying it to themselves, listening to the sound of it. They all liked it, to say the least, and before long they were chanting it in unison.

"*Nuke, Nuke, Nuke*," they chanted.

One time Coach fed Luis a ball, but he put his hand up and buckled over laughing. The ball went right by him, but Phooder didn't count it. When the *Love Machine* finally composed himself again, Phooder gave him an easy feed, just like you'd expect, and Lopez drove me deep into the corner and approached the net on the first shot. I was on the defensive right away. It hurt my heels running on my bare feet and I couldn't move quickly enough to make an offensive play. I hit a slice at his feet and he handled it, putting me on the run to the other corner. I got to it, but I had to throw up a lob. It was too short. He pounded it away for a winner.

I won't go into it too much except to say that I did it. I took off my underwear and ran the sprint with my balls dangling. I was chilly and my penis was shriveled up and small. Everyone tried to slap my ass with their racquets each time I came back to the baseline and a bunch of times they got me with the frame instead of the strings. As you can imagine, it didn't feel good and I didn't find it humorous like everyone else in the gym. I knew I was kind of thin and funny looking with my clothes off, but I didn't realize it was that obvious.

"*Nuke, Nuke, Nuke*," they shouted.

. . .

That night Melody showed up at my room with a condom in her hand. She clasped her hands around the back of my neck, pecked me on the lips, and said, "I'm ready. I want to make love to you."

Coach Phooder had let us out of practice right after everyone finished watching me run the suicide. I had dressed and gone straight to my dorm without talking to anyone. I skipped dinner because I didn't want to see or talk to anybody. The team always ended up sitting together in the cafeteria, and there was no way I was going to face that. If my own mother had called, I don't think I would have talked to her. Mel was the only person in the world who could have reached me, and here she was with a condom in her hand.

She hugged me and I hugged her back. We stood there in a prolonged embrace and when she started running her hands over me sensually—up and down my hips and around in front on my chest—it struck something inside of me.

"Oh, Wilson," she said.

There is something that happens to me that I've come to identify and understand somewhat since that time. It's this strange thing where, when something happens where I feel rejected or traumatized, there's a kind of firing inside of me. That's how I'd describe it: *a firing*. This was one of the first times I remember it happening. I was feeling freakish, rejected, alone from the Nuke incident. That triggered things.

It's quite odd when you think about it. Here I was with the woman who had been voted, in Phooder's words, *number one most fuckable*, and I was feeling skinny, bony, freakish, like a *Nuke*, I suppose, whatever that is. There was something about all the things that had been happening with the team in combination with the memories—disturbing and violent memories from my early life, many of them—that set me off when she started touching me sexually. I started sobbing.

"Make love to me," she said.

It was all very untimely because obviously she thought I was crying because I loved her and because I was about to have sex for the first time. I did love her and I did want to have sex, but it wasn't going to be my first time. And I have to admit that at that moment I was crying for myself because of what had happened in the gym and because of the memories, not for Melody and me.

You have to consider how unusual it was for someone her age, with her appearance, to still be a virgin. She had told me a number of times that she was saving herself. Perhaps because she was never valued in other ways, her sexuality, her virginity, became something she was very protective of. It was more than just sex she was offering me. For some reason she trusted me. She wanted to give herself to me.

She unbuttoned my shirt and ran her hands all over my belly and chest. She unzipped my pants and led me over to my mattress, which I kept on the floor. We were kissing and breathing heavily and she kept saying, "Make love to me, please, Wilson." Of course I should have stopped it then. I should have told her I wasn't a virgin. But I didn't. Instead, I did what she was asking. I made love to her.

I've tried to convince myself since then that it was beautiful, but it wasn't. Not at all. She told me to come on top, which made me feel almost like I was violating her. While I was on top of her, making love to her, I heard in my head the pathetic sound of the team cheering me on. They were chanting, but this time they weren't making fun of me. They were rooting for me. *"Nuke,*

Nuke, Nuke," they were saying. I couldn't help it, they were just there in my head. I felt grotesque.

I could see it was hurting her. Obviously she didn't enjoy it at all. She bled all over the sheets of my dorm room bed, and you can guess what that made me think of: Phooder chewing on his Milky Way making his filthy comment, "I'll bet *I* can make her bleed."

After we had sex, we lay there holding each other without speaking. She had started crying, but she calmed down in my arms. I was feeling all kinds of things. Pain and fear from the memories. Love for Melody. Anger at Coach Phooder and Luis. Guilt for not telling Mel. Guilt for making her bleed.

"I'm not a virgin," I said to her.

I don't know why I thought it was suddenly the time to tell her. What I do know is that I was very confused.

"Neither am I . . . anymore," she said, smiling shyly.

"I mean before, I wasn't," I said.

I felt her body go rigid and I felt her hold her breath in. Her heartbeat accelerated and the skin on her chest, underneath my cheek and ear, started to warm.

She sat up and pulled the sheets up over her breasts and stared at the wall.

"Get out, now, please," she said calmly.

Her voice was trembling and she was about to start crying. We were in my dorm room, of course, but I didn't argue with her.

"Get out, *please,*" she said.

The way I saw it, I needed to give her space. I had no choice but to leave my own room. I put on my boxer shorts and went down the hall to the shared bathroom for my floor. It was a men's dorm and, like nearly every men's bathroom I've seen, it was filthy and disgusting. I walked to the sink and turned the spigot on. There was a thin film of tiny black specks in the washbasin—

someone's whiskers—so I turned it off again and moved to another one. There were a few long blond hairs on that one, so I moved again. The one on the end was the cleanest. I rinsed my hands with hot water and then I turned the water cold, cupped my hands, and splashed water on my face. The door opened and Luis Lopez came in. He lived in my wing.

"Nuke," he said, without smiling.

He was wearing only boxer shorts, silk paisley ones.

"Nice job," he said.

I wondered if he had heard Mel and me.

He stared at me until I acknowledged him and then he smirked and tipped his chin. "For a while I thought it was going to be me getting naked." He stared at me, expressionless. "Fucking Phooder is nuts," he said.

He got his toothbrush and toothpaste from the little wooden shelves next to the door and set up in front of the same sink I had gone to first, the one with the whisker residue.

"I fucking hate this." He shook his head, took a step back, and gestured with his toothbrush at the basin. "Fucking pigs. Why are men such pigs?" he said.

He shifted to the sink with the long blond hairs. They didn't seem to bother him. He started brushing his teeth.

"How's your girlfriend?"

I stared at him while he brushed. White paste leaked out the side of his mouth.

"Didn't I see her going into your room?" he said.

I tore off a paper towel and started drying my face. He spit out his toothpaste and shook his head and stared at me.

"She's a nugget," he said.

I went out of the bathroom and back down the hallway to my dorm room. I listened for Melody crying, but I didn't hear anything. I knocked softly and still didn't hear her, so I went in. She was dressed and gathering up her things.

"I'm sorry," I said, but she pretended I hadn't said anything. She stuffed her purse in a little knapsack she had brought along. "I'm very sorry. I love you," I said.

She went over and stared at the bloody sheets on my mattress for a few moments and then she turned around and looked at my feet. She glanced up at my face and then she looked quickly down again. "Please don't try to talk to me," she said. "Don't ever try to talk to me," she said.

For a long time I thought life was easy for Melody. I mean, I always knew that being paraded around next to livestock could have some negative effect, but I guess I never realized *how much of an effect* it had. Now I'm sitting here thinking back over everything and remembering all of the *negative* things Melody told me about her adolescence. I always heard them and considered them and they were even part of what made me feel love and compassion for her, but now all of the difficult aspects of her early years are lining up neatly in my head.

Like the morning of the homecoming parade, in eleventh grade, when she found a partially decomposed rat in her locker. It was wrapped in a plastic bag with a red bow tied around the top. *Queen Henderson,* it said, on a tasteful card taped to the outside of the bag. The front of the card was a watercolor painting of a pale-skinned woman with a sun umbrella, fanning herself. A freshman boy who had his locker next to hers offered, chivalrously, to get rid of it for her. It stank up the whole east wing, Mel told me, and there was a crowd around her section of lockers holding their noses and giggling. "It was in my locker, it's mine to throw away," she told the boy as she carried the rat down the hallway and out to the Dumpster with everyone staring at her.

And there was the night she was out with some friends in her father's Ford Pinto. (These things happened to her before we met, but she told me about them.) When she and her friends came out of the movie, there were three human feces on the hood. Apparently, some misdirected teenagers' idea of irony—turds on the hood of the homecoming queen's car. They were definitely "fresh human poops," she told me, and there was no question in her mind that she was targeted. She drove that car to school *every* day, *everyone* knew it was hers. "No question," she said.

And things happened with women, too. In junior high, the day after Danny Hoffman asked her out, two girls on the field hockey team tried to beat her up behind the school. They came up behind her and tripped her, hooked her shins with their hockey sticks. "We'll see if Danny wants you after this," they said, apparently intending to affect her beauty by beating her. I'd almost never heard of that, jealous girls taking vengeance physically. Fortunately, with her speed, Mel was able to make a run for it and escape with only a bruise on her chin and a small cut on her face.

Women with whom she tried to cultivate friendships were always rejecting her. The assumption was that because she was beautiful, she was unintelligent. But Mel wasn't stupid. She was smart and very sensitive and it must have hurt her deeply, even more deeply than the pranks. It's one thing to get dead animals in your locker from mindless adolescent boys, but it's another to be rejected by people of the same sex whom you like and respect, people with whom you want to be friends.

. . .

It's difficult to explain how it is that Mel and I ended up together because I don't understand it completely myself. I know that when we started trying to make it work again, I considered, at least to some degree, the hard parts of her childhood, and that warmed me up to her. I know that I felt very bad about how it happened in my dorm and that I wanted to make it up to her. In the years after that incident, she was ruthless with me. She used words like "violated" and "robbed" to describe her loss of virginity. More than once, she ended up beating on my chest with her fists. I wasn't certain why she had come back to me and wanted to get back together, except, I supposed, that she loved me, and I found that wonderfully compelling. At some point, in the midst of all of the guilt and the drama, I made up my mind that I would be the first person to love her for something besides her appearance. (Even her own parents, when she was a child, bought her makeup kits and encouraged her to enter the contests.) I think I thought I owed it to her. Even if what I saw inside of her was unappealing—even if it was desperate, lacking self-esteem, vicious, self-preserving—I would love it back to health. But that is another self-deceit. It's one that, God knows, I learned much too late in life. It's a *deceit,* the notion that you can save something or someone. It's a *lie,* the idea that, by sacrificing yourself, you can make better what is broken. But that is what I believed. I was taught some of it in church, by the same summer Bible camp preachers who made me think my penis would fall off if I had premarital sex. There was Christ, the divine sacrifice. If you loved and cared for someone, that is what you did: you sacrificed yourself until they loved you again or until you healed what was broken inside of them.

Mel and I were together off and on through the rest of our college years. Somewhere in all of that confusion, for some strange reason, we started thinking that getting married would be good for us. We were married the fall after I graduated in grand, sentimental style—complete with flower children, the Wedding Song, and a white dress not unlike the one she wore for the Dairy Princess contest.

It's also hard for me to explain what happened during our four years of marriage, because, frankly, I don't understand that very well, either. I know we fought a lot. I know there was a lot of yelling, a lot of blaming for things that happened years before. I know that the sex was rarely good, that if I felt pleasure, if I let loose, I'd end up feeling uncomfortable, almost guilty. I know that I tried *very* hard to make it work between us. She cheated on me once and I felt I owed it to her to forgive. So I did.

It's also true that during our marriage she tried very hard to shuck the image of the beauty queen. She quit wearing makeup. Whenever she could, she dressed in ways that didn't flatter herself. She got furious with me if I so much as implied that she wear something I thought she looked sexy in. All the new friends she made were tough, hard-assed personalities, people who loathed superficiality. She tried to cultivate her inner self, to do things that she thought would add substance to her being. She got a master's in psychology. She counseled rape victims.

I've been delaying telling you what happened to Melody, because I wanted to explain how, since I've found out, I've been thinking and rethinking everything. I've been trying to figure out what role I had in it.

It was just last week. She called me and asked me out for coffee. "Sure," I said. I'm happy to be friends. It's good and healing to be friends. "How about tomorrow?" she asked, sounding rushed. "That's great. Tomorrow's great," I said, a little puzzled.

I had heard through one of our mutual friends that she wasn't doing that well and I had phoned her numerous times, but I always got her machine and she never returned my calls. I had heard that, among other things, she was living somewhat promiscuously, getting drunk all the time and sleeping with guys she didn't even care about. That wasn't the Mel I knew, but I figured that she was just hurting, going through a kind of a stage, or that she had changed, which was okay, too, of course.

I arrived early at the coffee shop where we had agreed to meet, and ordered, for myself, the kind of herbal tea I remembered was her favorite. I was feeling nostalgic—no romantic hopes, I was just sentimental at the idea of seeing and talking with her again. As I sipped the tea, glanced around at the interesting-looking people, and listened to the opera they had playing, I found myself full of hope. I was believing that Mel and I could be friends again—just friends, that's all, but the thought of it pleased me. I felt peaceful. I was glad she had phoned me.

The woman who served my tea was pleasant. She smiled when I asked for more hot water, and said, "Absolutely, let me bring it out to you." I felt slightly attracted to her—just in a superficial kind of way—and I thought, *Things are working out. Mel and I did the right thing. Soon I'll even feel like dating again.* I read the arts page of the newspaper for a few minutes and then I put it down. I put both hands around my teacup to keep them warm like I remembered Mel used to do and I sat there peacefully.

I saw her coming through the window of the coffee shop. At first I didn't even know for certain if it was her. Her hair was short, disheveled, and blond. In the time I knew her, she had never colored her hair, but on this day it was definitely blond. She had bleached it. She had on tight jeans, a tight white T-shirt, and a black leather vest with fringe. I saw all of those things first. She was walking with her head down. Her face was in the shadows.

"You like my hair?" she said, coming toward the table. "I was always a blonde at heart, wasn't I?"

I didn't say anything at first. I just stared at her face and tried to convince myself that what I was seeing wasn't real. It was too awful to do anything but stay calm, switch into crisis mode.

"I did it myself," she said, sitting down across from me. "Do you like it?" She tilted her head to the side, making her sarcasm obvious.

There were slits, open wounds, starting an inch or two below her eyes and extending all the way down her cheeks below the corners of her mouth. There was dried blood along the sides, and I couldn't believe, as fresh and open as they looked, that the slits weren't bleeding right then. You could tell the wounds were fresh, not older than twenty-four hours.

"Do you like it or not?" she said, not smiling, her eyebrows raised.

It was bizarre how things went off inside me at that moment. Some of the things were things you'd expect me to think of. I thought of Coach Phooder, Luis Lopez, and everyone shouting *Nuke* at me. I thought of Mel lying fetal in bed with the soft comforter I had bought for her next to her pale skin. I thought of the roaches in our apartment the fall we separated. I thought about Marianne Connely, what it felt like to have her between my legs. I thought of Mel in my dorm room, the blood on the sheets . . .

I guess it was some of the other things that fired inside of me that I found surprising. Again, that's how I'd describe it: *a firing,* a blipping of seemingly unrelated things: the deer that jumped out in front of my car and tried to run on its broken forelegs, blood on the support beams in my friend's basement, images of my father after he was burned, his charred, swollen head, his little stubs for hands . . .

I must have checked out for thirty seconds or so. Apparently I was staring beyond her, over her head, out the window or somewhere, because she waved her hand in front of my face violently and beat on the table with her fist.

"Hello, I'm here," she said.

I looked back at her and shook my head and said, *"My God, Melody."*

I reached out to touch her hand, which was still clenched on the table in a fist, but she yanked it back and laughed diabolically. She shook her head and said, "Don't touch me, don't ever try to touch me." I stared at her as she stormed out of the coffee shop in the same way she had stormed out of my dorm room years before.

I found out later what she had done. I mean, I had already figured at the coffee shop that she had cut herself, but I only found out for certain afterwards when I called our friends.

I don't know what all goes on inside someone, what kind of pain and anger they must be in to engage in that kind of self-mutilation, but in a very strange way it doesn't completely surprise me about Melody. I understand that the revenge she was taking wasn't just against me, but it's still hard not to feel that way, it's still hard not to feel like I've also been mutilated. It's been almost two weeks since she cut herself, and from what I am told, she is doing surprisingly well. She is in good hands. She is with a bunch of our mutual friends. She's had some kind of plastic surgery that will help make the scarring less obvious, but it will still be very visible. I tried to visit her earlier this week when she was in the hospital overnight. I called into her room from the nurses' station to tell her I was there, and a few of our friends happened to be in with her at the time. They met me outside her room, in the hallway, asked me if I "didn't think it was time I leave her alone." These were our very good friends, you understand—our *mutual* friends.

I've been skipping work the last few days, sleeping in, wandering in and out of coffee shops and bars. I've spent a few evenings with some new friends that I've made here and I've tried explaining it to them, but they aren't like Mel's and my old friends. I don't know what I expect of them, they don't really know me very well. I would probably look at them strangely, too, if I heard them say some of the things I've said in the last few days.

Today I'm going fishing, I've decided. It's very male of me, I realize, but I'm doing it anyway because I'm in pain and I don't know what else to do. I'm tired of sitting around here racking my brain. I'm tired of feeling guilt for everything. I realize I'm guilty, but I also realize, or maybe I've decided, that we're all guilty: me, Coach Phooder, Luis Lopez, Mel's high school boyfriends, her jealous and ruthless girlfriends, the bastards who paraded her around with animals, her parents for buying her makeup kits and entering her in the contests, even Melody. We all scarred her, but now she has scarred herself, too. Anyway, who am I to patronize? She has had surgery, she has our friends, she will heal. I am alone here in this stupid town, and the way I feel now, I wonder if I will ever heal.

But then, who am I to feel pity for myself or for anyone? And who am I to patronize her? Who am I to assume that she wasn't right in doing what she did? Maybe it's sexist of me. Maybe I'm putting too much emphasis on her physical beauty. Who knows? Maybe now she'll be better off. Maybe now she'll finally be free from all she hated about being what we made her into. Maybe now she'll finally be free from what she was on that Dairy Princess Polaroid.

My God I loved her, my God I'm sorry, my dear Melody, the beauty queen!

Part II

Golf

My father's nose and ears were burned away and his head swelled up three times. He could hear, but couldn't speak. Once, before he died, an old colleague of his came in past the nurses' station in the ICU and found his bed. The man told him they'd play golf again in a few weeks. But his hands and feet were gone. They were burnt to little stubs.

Flying

First let me tell you that eight years ago my father crashed his plane. It was a low-winged twin-engine plane—very difficult for an amateur pilot to negotiate—and it's no wonder that when his left engine failed during takeoff, he was unable to get the plane up and out. He nearly did, onlookers said, but the tail caught power lines a half-mile from the runway and the fuselage ignited. The plane went up in flames. So did he. He ran from the wreckage on fire. The plane had skidded into the parking lot of an outdoor farmers' market and the stand holders, mostly Amish and Mennonites, just gazed at him, dumbfounded, while he rolled around on the ground to put out the fire consuming his skin. Then, having extinguished most of the flames, he stood up and swore at the cluster of peace-loving Anabaptists. "Don't just stand there like a bunch of fucking pacifists! Get me water! Do something, *anything*!" he screamed. A

Mennonite woman who witnessed the crash and came to visit my father in the hospital before he died told me these things. "Your father tried to orchestrate his own rescue," she said.

My father was a businessman. He was always orchestrating, organizing, managing things. His children were not exempted from the list of things that he thought needed managing. To say it mildly, I resisted it. I resisted him. He was never much of a father to me. He was of a mind—the same stubborn mind he had when he ran from the wreckage and swore at the Amish and Mennonites—that the world is a cold, unforgiving place. He resolved to, if nothing else, impart that knowledge to his children. He spoke to me often the cliché, "Willie, nobody's going to do anything for you. If you want something in this world you're going to have to get up off your ass and get it yourself." People *are not* good, was his basic belief. And, beyond their moral position in the world—perhaps even worse, in his view—people didn't really *act,* they didn't act with decision. People, he thought, lacked *initiative.*

But he was still my father and for whatever differences we had, it still wasn't nice to see him suffer on his deathbed. It wasn't nice to see his ears burnt off, his head swollen up like a balloon, or his hands charred and shriveled into what looked like little chicken's paws. In the weeks after the accident, we had to decide whether or not to pull the plug. The doctors told us, "Statistically he has no chance to live. And, if he does live, he'll be severely disfigured, *severely* disfigured." Of course we chose not to pull the plug. Of course he died anyway—after four or five weeks of unnecessary suffering.

This Christmas I found myself, for reasons I didn't completely understand, listless, unmotivated, lacking initiative. I found myself possessing, in generous proportion, all of the qualities my father hated. It's true that my life has been difficult in some ways. My parents divorced when I was young, I've since lost a parent, I've been through a divorce of my own, I've lost a couple of close friends to accidents, failed at more than one career path. But when I get like this I blame no one but myself. I have nothing to complain about. I've been fortunate in many ways. I'm healthy. I'm alive. I'm surviving.

But what do you do with Christmas? What do you do at age thirty-four, in your hometown, out of work, divorced, no children, almost no remaining unmarried friends? What do you do with Christmas and the time couched between it and New Year's?

My mother has moved to Florida, remarried. I have a sibling here in Reading, but he has his own family. There are other friends I could have called, but they have their own lives.

It was the afternoon of Christmas Eve. Everyone was bustling in and out of the shops, buying gifts for one another, toys for their children. I was walking up and down Main Street, staring in at the displays. I saw it hanging in one of the windows. A remote-control plane. A low-winged twin engine. It looked like a Piper Cub. It looked just like my father's plane.

"How much is that plane?" I said, overexcited, to the obese gray-haired woman behind the counter.

"Which? That one there?" she said.

She slid her thick glasses up on her nose and leaned her head back as she looked up at the plane. She was smoking and eating one of the Christmas cookies that were displayed on the counter for customers.

"Oh, Jesus, I ain't know about that one," she said.

Another woman was seated beside her, also smoking and eating holiday baked goods.

"You know what we're taking for that RC plane?" she said to the second woman.

"That Billy's old plane, ain't it?"

"Been hanging there since kingdom come."

"He built that after the accident, ain't he? That's an old one. I ain't even know if it runs."

The large, gray-haired woman to whom I had first talked leaned her head forward.

"I can help you with the models, trains and that." She pointed over her shoulder at nothing in particular. "But my boy Billy does the RC." She winked at me. "Yeah, RC's Billy's area," she said.

She looked at the other woman, who had set down her cigarette and was now dipping her cookie in a hot, steaming drink. "Where's that Billy gone off to?" she said to her.

Both of them took bites of their Christmas cookies and chewed.

"Billy!" the first woman yelled, leaning back in her chair. "Billy!" She borrowed a puff off the other woman's cigarette. "There ain't nothing wrong with his ears—or he can hear fine with them, at least," she said, looking at the other woman, chuckling. She exhaled smoke. "He'll be coming out," she said.

While I waited, I looked around the hobby shop at the available merchandise. There were slot cars, trains, little rubber tires to go on remote-control cars, glues and balsa woods of all shapes and sizes. The shop was in disarray. Many of the models and kits looked old and dusty. The trains were mixed in with the remote-control cars, the glues and balsa wood were scattered all over the shelves, randomly.

"Here's your man," one of the women behind the counter said. "Billy, this man interested in your plane," she said.

He considered me.

"You fly?" he said.

He spoke in a kind of high-pitched, almost falsetto voice that sounded very strange. But that wasn't the first thing you noticed about him. The skin on most of his neck and face was a grotesque, purplish-red pigment. It had small white spots interspersed on it. He was wearing a baseball cap which he wore as low as he could on his head, but you could see that most of his right ear was missing. I had met plenty of other burn survivors, as they call themselves, visiting my father in the burn unit before he died. This man was a survivor himself. These were burn scars.

"That one up there," I said, trying not to stare. I pointed at the plane. "How much is that one?" I asked.

He had been looking down, somewhat nervously, to this point and when he realized which plane I wanted, he looked up at me and smiled tentatively. His lips had been burned, too, they were the same strange purple shade. They looked dry and shrunken, like he wanted to spread them out wider on his face, but was unable to.

"That ain't really for sale. That's the first plane I ever builded," he said.

"It looks like a Piper Cub replica."

He smiled again and looked down at the floor shyly like I had exposed him somehow. Obviously his skin couldn't redden, but it was as if he was blushing.

"Yeah? You got one?" he said.

"My father had one."

"He still got it?"

I wasn't sure how to answer the question.

"No, he crashed it," I said.

He shook his head slowly, but kept smiling.

"Too bad, they're good ones to fly, the twin engines. They're fast ones," he said.

The woman I had first talked to offered me a Christmas cookie, but I declined. She seemed put off. She peered at me while she put a cigarette in her mouth, lit a match, and held the cigarette over the flame.

"Billy, that man gonna buy your plane or what?" she said. "You ain't gonna stand there shooting the shit all Christmas Eve. We ain't taking less than three hundred for it."

The woman was apparently his mother, though the man appeared, himself, to be well into his thirties.

"She's worth at least that," he said proudly. "But I hadn't been figuring on selling it."

He had turned his head to address the woman, and when he looked back at me, I realized I had been staring at the flesh on the side of his head that had once been his ear. He pulled his baseball cap down every so often to cover it, but the sinewy flesh was still visible.

"You got a plane now?"

"No, I don't," I said.

He pushed his glasses up on his face and surveyed me. The glasses had fallen crooked on his nose and I realized it was because they were resting too low on the right side of his face, that they had slipped down over the area where his ear should have been.

"You had your own plane before, though, ain't you?" he said.

"I haven't," I said.

He touched the back of his baseball cap, adjusted it lower on his head.

"You flown before, though, ain't you?"

"No, not exactly," I said.

My answer to this question seemed to puzzle, almost disturb

him. He adjusted his glasses again, looked down, and started rubbing the back of his neck.

"You ain't flied?"

"No, I haven't, but I'd like to learn. I'd like to learn to fly that one up there," I said, pointing at the Piper Cub like my father's in the display.

He kept looking down. He seemed ashamed for me, personally embarrassed for my lack of experience.

"It ain't easy flying, I'll tell you that. Specially not a low-winged twin-engine. Specially not if you never flied before," he said.

He met my eyes for a moment, and then he looked up at the plane wistfully. He started shaking his head.

"I ain't know. I ain't even know if she runs," he said.

He looked back at me and stared. I waited for him to speak again, to tell me what my options were, but he just stared at me through his thick, wire-rimmed glasses. After a few seconds he took the glasses off and rubbed his eyes. I noticed then, for the first time, that he didn't have eyebrows or eyelashes.

"What kind of other planes do you have in here?" I finally said, looking up at the higher, half-empty shelves.

He pointed out a couple of models, but he explained that they all took at least a week to assemble.

"I was hoping to fly tomorrow," I said.

"Tomorrow?"

I nodded.

"Christmas Day?"

"Yeah," I said.

He studied me.

"You ain't got a meal or nothing to go to?"

He seemed as much engaged by this fact as confused.

"Not really," I said, shrugging.

He looked around the store, glanced over at the women behind the counter for a moment, and then stared up at the plane. He seemed to be considering something carefully.

"I don't even know if that thing runs," he said, looking distraught, shaking his head again. He looked distraught. "You ain't gonna be flying Christmas. There just ain't no way," he said.

He gave me a beat-up catalog from behind the counter that had pictures, specifications, and spare parts for remote-control planes. He told me to study it, figure out what I wanted, then come back to him. He said he'd order it all for me after the holidays.

"It's gonna be close to a month till you're in the air," he said.

I gave him the phone number of the place I was staying for the next couple of weeks.

"Give me a call if you come into any used planes," I told him.

As I headed toward the door, the women behind the counter offered me a cookie again. I took it this time. They wished me a Merry Christmas. I smiled mildly, wished them one too, waved at the man who had helped me with planes.

Back out in the street, it felt even colder than it had been before. I'd only been in the shop for ten or fifteen minutes, but in that time the sun had already descended. It was getting dark. I browsed the shops for a little while longer. I went in and out of a few, but mostly I just gazed at the displays. When the shops started to close down, I got myself to a grocery store. I was going to be staying in by myself, but it was Christmas Eve and I decided I should have some kind of a special dinner. I bought one of those rotisserie chickens that you wonder about, the ones you always see spinning and simmering in supermarkets behind hot glass. I bought a few potatoes to mash, some frozen broccoli, and, at the last minute, threw in some eggs and nutmeg to make eggnog. They had phone cards at the register for a discounted Christmas rate. I bought one of those to call my mother in Florida, since she didn't have the phone number of where I was staying. I was sleeping at a friend's house, watching over it until he and his family got back from their three-week vacation.

I did talk to my mother that evening. She and her new husband were enjoying their first Christmas together so she was a little distracted on the phone, but we had a nice conversation. I called one or two other friends and it was the same kind of thing. They were glad to hear from me, but there was commotion in the background, eager children waiting to open up their gifts. I had some trouble getting to sleep, but I got up out of bed and drank enough of my eggnog—added some extra rum to it—that I was able to doze off.

The next morning I let myself sleep. I didn't try to get up at the crack of dawn. There was no reason to. I didn't have a tree or presents waiting under it for me or any of my loved ones. I don't smoke regularly, but my friend had a pack on hand, so I stood by myself, puffing, looking out across the fields of an Amish farm that bordered the property. It was a cornfield. There were rows of frozen, broken corn stalks extending as far as I could see. I tried to imagine what the field looked like in the summer when the corn was tall, lush, and green.

As I stood there on the porch, staring at the frozen brown field, I heard the ring of the phone, faintly, inside. I was certain it wasn't for me—it wasn't my house—but I ran to answer it anyway.

"You ready?" the voice on the other end said.

"Ready for what? Who is this?" I said.

"I got her running. I got her running just now," he said.

I had left the catalog in my back seat and given up on the idea of flying so it didn't register at first, but the high-pitched tone of the voice gave it away. It was the man from the hobby shop. I had given him the number.

"Listen, listen to this," he said.

There was a brief pause, and then I heard one of the engines start up.

"You hear that?" he said, shouting over it.

"I hear it."

"Let's go. Let's do it," he said.

"Do what? What are you talking about?"

"Let's do it. Let's get her in the air."

"What? Now?" I said.

"You doing anything?"

I thought about the question.

"No, not exactly," I said.

"Well, let's do it, let's get her flying."

He told me to meet him at a place where I hadn't been since I was a kid. He called it the Old Route 48, but it had different names: the Lost Highway, the Goat Path, Jacob's Trail. It was a state highway through Amish farmland that was abandoned before it was paved. The ground had been bulldozed, built up and leveled off—the bridges and underpasses had even been erected—but the road was never finished. There had been so much backlash from the Amish and from other groups lobbying to protect the land that the project was aborted. It was left unpaved.

He described one of the old bridges to me and told me to meet him there. I knew right where it was. I remembered it. In ninth grade, I had had a sixteen-year-old girlfriend who drove me there with her to smoke Virginia Slims, drink Boone's strawberry wine, and make out beneath the underpass. My girlfriend and I preferred the name Jacob's Trail because, on the occasion of our first bottle of Boone's, we encountered the man from whom that name had come. He had long gray hair and a bushy gray beard with no mustache. He would walk along the abandoned highway bellowing hymns in German. We had heard about him. The story was that he was Amish and that he had been excommunicated from the church, that he lived in a shack by himself somewhere along the abandoned highway. That day, he saw us sitting under one of the bridges and he stopped, glared at us for a while, and then started barking apocalyptic curses: *"You have wandered onto the place they call Jacob's Trail. It is written: God's people shall cast you out from among them. They shall cast you out into darkness. You shall be condemned to the abandoned highway. You shall be condemned to Jacob's Path,"* he said, laughing diabolically, and then breaking into song again. I drove the same back road we used to take to get there when I was in high school. I parked along the road as far off as I could get without putting my tire in the ditch. I hiked the half-mile back to the old highway and walked up on the heightened level platform of grass where the pavement would have been.

At first, I didn't see the man from the shop. I stood there staring down the desolate, unfinished highway, reminiscing about my adolescent years. I mused about the significance—or insignificance—of my adolescent girlfriend and I thought about the shunned Amish man. I wondered if he still lived along the path, or if, as with most childhood memories, he had passed on. It was cold and breezy—I thought almost too breezy—to fly a model plane.

After a few moments, my trance was interrupted by, somewhere above me, the faint hum of an engine. I tilted my head back and looked to my left and my right. I didn't see anything, but I did hear the buzz of the RC plane's engine. The sound got louder and louder and then, before I knew what was happening, the plane whizzed by only twenty or thirty feet from my head. It ascended, did a circle and loop, and landed a couple of hundred feet in front of where I was standing. The man from the store came up onto the elevated grass highway, holding the controls. He taxied the plane to his feet, reached down and shut off the engine. He walked toward me, smiling. I noticed his restrained, thin-lipped grin again. It looked like his skin was too tight, like it stretched the skin on his face, like smiling caused him physical pain.

I squatted down and looked at the Piper Cub. On the ground like this, it looked much bigger than it had in the air or when it was hanging in the display. It must have had a three-foot wingspan. Everything right down to the maroon pinstriping was meticulously crafted. The stripes started at the nose, went out the wings, back in again, and all the way back to the fuselage. I realize now that I was blinded by the beauty of that machine. I've checked pictures since that time and I know this isn't the case, but at that moment I felt convinced that my father's plane had precisely the same maroon pinstriping. On the back of the body near the tail, it said, in cursive, *Billy's Dream*.

"How long did it take you to build this thing?" I said.

"A couple months for the body. I did extra on it, though, you know, with all the detailing and that." With the airplane controls in his hand, he sounded more confident, almost outgoing. "Took another couple months to get the engines in. To get her so she wasn't yawing, you know. It's tricky with the twin-engines, getting them balanced," he said.

I kept kneeling over the plane, admiring it, touching it delicately. He was considering something soberly.

"I built this one in my first months back from the hospital. It was the first thing I really did after the accident."

I waited for him to talk more about whatever it was that he was referring to, but I didn't respond right away. I didn't want to say the wrong thing. I didn't want to say anything intrusive.

We stood in silence for ten or twenty seconds, staring out across the Amish farmland.

"How long ago was that?" I finally asked. The question seemed not too personal, yet showed I was interested.

"Six years now," he said.

It had been seven and a half since my father died.

We stood there in silence a little longer, and while we did I noticed something about him that I find it hard to believe I didn't notice the first time I met him. He had little stubs for fingers on his left hand. He was holding the controls to the plane with what there was of that hand, sort of resting it on his forearm. One of his fingers was gone, two of them had a single joint, and the other two—one of them his thumb—had no joint at all. They had been burnt to little stubs.

"So you ain't never flown," he said.

"No, I haven't."

He had had the remote control pinned to his chest with the forearm of his damaged hand, but to show me how to run it, he shifted it to his other hand, which wasn't scarred and appeared to be fully functional.

"This is the throttle here," he said.

His voice was so high it made me wonder if it had been damaged.

"You gotta do it gradual on the takeoff or the nose'll dive, the props'll hit the ground," he said.

He pinched the throttle knobs between two of the partial fingers of his scarred hand.

"Gradually, like this," he said, moving the joystick slowly.

The plane's engines weren't running so it was safe for him to hand me the controls to practice with.

"This controls the wings—and the lift off the tail. They run on rechargeables—on batteries. See it moving there on the wings?" he said, pointing. He paused for a moment, considering me. "You know anything about planes?" he said.

"A little bit," I said.

"You know how they steer? How the wind rushes under the wings, makes them lift?"

I nodded at him. "I think so," I said, though I didn't really understand.

He reached over with his good hand and moved the controls around.

"See how the one flap goes up while the other'n goes down? That's how they steer," he said.

He crouched down next to the plane.

"All right, now we gonna test your flying skill. Turn left," he said.

I looked back and forth from the plane to my remote control and followed his directions.

"Now turn right," he said. "Good. Now give her some lift, like you're taking off."

This part was more confusing. At first, I pushed the joystick upward, which was wrong, apparently.

"You just done a nosedive. Other way," he said. "Down for up. Just like a real plane."

Remember that this was December 25 and while there was no snow on the ground, it was very cold. My hands were getting numb. I blew on them so I could feel them well enough to handle the controls. When he spoke again, I noticed his breath was visible. It looked like smoke.

"Down for up, remember that," he said.

He went down over the slope, off the grass highway, for a few moments and then reappeared carrying a black leather bag. The bag looked like an antique doctor's case from the mid-1900s. It was old, weathered, stylish. He carried it over to the plane, dug around in it, and pulled out some odd-looking accessories. One of them was an electric-powered rubber tool that fit over the airplane's props—to get them spinning and start up the engines.

"Let's get her flying," he said.

He pinned the plane down with his maimed hand and he fit the tool over one of the propellers. The prop turned and the engine sputtered. He winced, scrunched up his nose at me, and tried it again. This time it started.

The plane moved, pulling to one side. He dropped the starting tool, grabbed the plane with his good hand, and waved wildly at me. He pointed with one of the single-jointed fingers of his scarred hand.

"Down, down," he said, shouting over the engine, his voice barely audible.

I was still holding the controls. I realized the throttle was halfway up. I turned it down.

"That's better!" he yelled.

He smiled his tight-skinned smile and nodded, and then he put the tool over the second engine's propeller. It fired up on the first try.

"Leave the lift in the middle, then pull back on it slightly as you accelerate," he shouted.

I didn't really understand what he was talking about, but I nodded anyway.

He walked the plane to the center of the grass highway and knelt down with it. Then he pointed the thumb of his scarred hand upward and screamed, "Now! Accelerate!"

I hadn't expected him to let me fly it.

"Don't you want to fly it?" I screamed.

"No, you!" he screamed back, shaking his head violently. "Accelerate!"

It was all happening very quickly. I was holding the controls, I didn't know what else to do. I moved the throttle slowly upward just as he had told me. The engines started screaming.

He let go of the plane and it took off up the grass runway. It started bouncing up and down like it was going to get up and out. He scrambled over next to me.

"Now! Give her lift. Pull back on the stick!" he screamed.

He held out his left hand next to my controls to demonstrate. He held it palm upward, stubs extended, and with his other hand, showed me the proper motion of the joystick.

"Down for up!" he screamed.

I pulled down on the controls as slightly as I could and the plane lifted off. It yawed, but stayed in the air. It ascended on the horizon, moving away from me.

He stood in front of me, knees bent, gyrating his hands upward as if he were conducting a symphony.

"Good! Higher! Good!" he said.

The plane continued ascending.

"Now level her off again," he said.

The plane, *Billy's Dream,* was far enough away now that he wasn't shouting anymore. In fact, he was speaking in a kind of a whisper, trying to calm me. He held out his hand like it was a remote again and he pushed up very slightly on his imaginary joystick, demonstrating.

"Up on the stick, just a little, to level her off," he said.

I did what he said and the plane leveled.

"Good, you got her, that's good, easy with her," he said.

I have to take the time now to tell you how it felt for the couple of moments I had that plane cruising along smoothly in the air. I have to tell you because it was like nothing I've ever felt before. Flying, I've come to believe, gives you a false sense of security. Understand that I had been up in a real airplane before—my father's airplane—but I never felt on those occasions anything that approached the elation I felt actually *controlling* this machine. *That* is what *flying* is, actually *controlling* an airplane. I've never felt the way I felt for the period of time I had that plane stable in the air. Strangely, or perhaps not so strangely, for a few moments while I flew it, I felt I understood something about my father I had never understood before. I felt I understood why my father flew airplanes—why he willingly took on the risk inherent in it. I even thought I felt something I almost never felt when he was alive. I felt close to him. It was as if I were inside the cockpit of this little RC plane and my father was seated next to me, supporting, even affirming me. I was soaring.

"You gotta turn it back to us. You're getting out of range," the man said.

He was still talking in a kind of a whisper, but a greater urgency had come into his voice. I didn't recognize it at the time, but it was an urgency that, looking back on it, seemed to say: *Don't be deceived by what you're feeling now. The beauty and security you feel at this moment are an illusion. There is a great risk to flying.*

I guess what happened next was that I got too forceful with the controls. I banked too hard into the turn. I should have been more gentle with it, like he'd been telling me. The plane turned one hundred and eighty degrees, but then it started climbing. Of course once I'd turned it, the airplane was facing me, and that reversed everything. Now, to go left, I had to push the stick to the right, and to go right, I had to push left. At the same time, *down for up,* and *up for down* didn't change. It still confuses me just thinking about it.

"Level it, level it," he said. His knees were bent and he was gesticulating like a composer again, but now he was motioning down instead of up.

I was panicked and confused. I pulled back on the joystick—the wrong direction—and the nose of the plane angled more sharply upward. It pointed directly into the air, like a rocket, tail at a right angle to the ground.

"That ain't right. The other way!" he screamed.

You may know how this works with planes. You may have seen it at air shows when they go straight up and stall the engines. If a winged flying machine ascends too sharply for too long, the effect, eventually, is that it reverses directions, goes nose-first into a tailspin. Well, that is what occurred at this moment with this man's meticulously crafted plane. I couldn't get it leveled off and then, suddenly, it was plummeting.

"She's tailing," he screamed, scrambling over to me. "Let go! Don't try to steer her!" he said.

I've found out since then that this is one of the things they teach when you learn to fly real planes: If you quit fighting the controls during a tailspin, sometimes the plane will straighten out on its own. But I didn't know anything about flying. I kept forcing it, fighting it, trying to correct my error. I kept pushing *down for up,* as he'd been telling me.

"Oh, Jesus, she's tailing," he said again, somehow both screaming and whining. "Gimme the controls! Gimme 'em!" he said.

I handed them to him, but he didn't get them pinned properly against his body with his maimed hand and they fell to the ground. He left the control unit there as he watched the plane plunge. He must have been waiting for the plane to right itself, but it never did. It hit the Lost Highway at full speed. *Billy's Dream* went up in flames.

. . .

I watched him, waiting for him to make a move toward the plane. In the commotion, his baseball cap had come off. His missing ear and the burn scars on his head were exposed. Little stubbles of hair grew on half of his head, but the hairless skin on the other half was that same leprous, reddish-purple. He stood there staring at the flames, slump shouldered, his breath visible, looking like smoke again.

"What should we do?" I asked him.

The plane had come down dangerously close to us, not more than thirty feet from where we were standing. He kept staring at the burning airplane.

I don't know what I thought I was going to accomplish, there was nothing left to save.

I made a movement toward the wreckage. He put up his hand.

"No, leave it," he said. "Ain't nothing you can do. Ain't nothing you can do once they burning."

Fighter

The surgeon spoke with his hands on the table, his fat fingers interlocked.

"You understand, if he lives, he'll be severely disfigured," he said.

"We understand."

"Severely disfigured."

"Yes."

"He's in great pain."

We nodded and stared at him.

"He may not have use of his hands. Statistically, he has no chance. He's off the charts." He looked at us over his glasses and

then he took them off and let them dangle from the string around his neck. He shook his head. "The grafts will go on for years. It's very expensive, very painful. It will take a miracle."

"He's very stubborn. He's a fighter. We believe," we said.

Daddy

I moved into an apartment up the street from my aging mother a couple of months ago. I've been working part-time, painting barns, and I've just been sort of drifting through the days. But a few weeks ago, on Thanksgiving Eve, Travis and Rudy and I were drinking a pitcher of beer at Smitty's Tavern when there was some commotion at the opposite end of the bar. The man was fairly old. Apparently a piece of roast beef had lodged itself in his throat. A woman beside him was calling for help and a small crowd was assembling. Nobody seemed to know what to do.

I was seated closest to that side so I got to the other end of the bar before my friends. The old man was already turning blue. There was one guy there trying to dislodge the piece of meat, but he wasn't getting it done. He had the old man buckled over at the waist with one hand and he was pounding on his back with the other, but he could barely support the choking man's weight.

"Oh my God, Dad, breathe," the woman shouted. "Somebody help him, he's going to die! Please!"

I didn't think about what I was doing. There was no time to think. No one else was stepping in. I came in from the side and I reached under the choking man's arms and took up his weight. The other guy stepped out of the way. I guess it hadn't occurred to me before I stepped in how heavy the old man would be. He was fairly large, bigger than me, and in order to do the Heimlich I had to hoist him up high enough to get my hands beneath his ribs and at the same time support his weight. He kept sliding down in my arms so my arms were around his rib cage instead of his gut. He felt like a warm corpse in my arms.

It didn't come out on the first couple of thrusts. I wasn't doing it very hard. I was worried about breaking his ribs.

"Jesus, he's blue. He's going to die," the woman shouted.

"You're not doing it right. You've got to get right under his sternum," another man yelled.

He was right. I didn't know what I was doing. I had read those posters you see in hospitals and diners about the Heimlich, but I had never taken first aid and I had certainly never performed the procedure on anyone myself. There were probably half a dozen other people in the bar who could do it better than me. I kept squeezing his gut, thrusting into him from behind. I started thinking, *My God, what have I gotten into? What if the guy dies in my arms?* I considered stepping away and letting someone else have a try.

I didn't, though. There was no time. I kept pumping my fists into his gut, and eventually, I guess, it started to work. The woman yelled to keep going, that it was coming up. I thought about reaching my hand into his mouth—I had seen my mother do that to a neighbor boy who had a seizure once—but I had both my arms around his midsection and it was all I could do to support his weight. After just a few more thrusts, the piece of meat spewed out onto the floor. The roast beef landed together with the bile or saliva or whatever it was in a tiny pool. I dragged the man toward a table near the bar and set him down on a chair. He hunched over and put his hands on his knees and wheezed. Someone asked him if he could breathe. He bobbed his head up and down. He took little breaths while he stared at the floor.

Most everyone else in the bar had gathered by this time, but the man seemed to be all right and I felt strange standing there, so I walked back to our table at the other end of the bar.

It was awkward sitting back down with Travis and Rudy. These were childhood friends of mine. Very good friends. They knew I didn't know first aid. I was glad that the situation worked out, but I felt presumptuous having stepped up.

My friend Rudy patted me on the back.

"Nice job, Will. Hero," he said, smirking.

I nodded and picked up my glass of beer. I was shaking so much I could hardly keep it steady at my lips.

"Who's got a cigarette?" I said.

My friend Travis handed me one.

"Is he okay?" he said.

"I think so."

"I guess he was in pretty bad shape," Rudy said.

"Yeah." I took another swig of my beer. "I'm just glad he didn't die in my arms," I said.

"That would have put a damper on the evening," Travis said.

We all laughed. I lit up my cigarette and the three of us took turns making jokes about the whole thing. About how much it would have sucked if he'd have croaked. About how I looked ramming him from behind.

After a while, an ambulance crew came in and took the old man out. They tried to put him on a stretcher, but he refused. I saw him stare at our table, at me, as they led him out by the arm.

One of the waitresses came over and had me write my name and number down on a pad. The old man's daughter was very grateful to me. She wanted my name and information. She wanted to make sure I was properly thanked.

We were starved by the time our own roast beef sandwiches finally arrived. We wolfed them down in just a few minutes, not talking as we ate. After a few more beers, my friend Rudy declared the roast beef "the best goddamn sandwich" he'd ever had. That made us all laugh again. We went on talking and drinking for a while and nobody mentioned what had happened until we went to leave. Then the waitress came and told us our whole tab was on the house.

"Ah, we'll take three more sandwiches and another pitcher of Rolling Rock, in that case," Rudy said, when she was just out of ear's reach.

We went to another bar and had a few more beers, and that was the last we talked about it the rest of the night. But I never stopped thinking about it. They dropped me off at my apartment. I plopped down on the couch and tried to fall asleep, but I lay awake there until almost 4:00 A.M. I woke up early the next morning and drank coffee until noon, staring out at the rain, wondering how the man was. I picked up my mother and we went to a relative's house for a turkey dinner. I thought about it there, too. I thought about the puddle of roast beef and bile while I ate bites of turkey.

That night, the man's daughter rang me up.

She seemed nervous on the phone. She explained to me how

the medical personnel had said that if it hadn't been for me, her father would have died. She said how thankful they both were. I found myself trying to put her at ease.

"Well, I was just at the right place at the right time," I said. "I'm just glad he's okay."

But then the old man came on the phone. He had apparently picked up in another part of the house. His voice was quivering.

"Are you the man that tried to save my life?" he said.

"Well, yes, I guess I am," I told him.

"Who the hell do you think you are?" he said.

"Daddy, hang up the phone," the daughter said from another part of the house.

"Who the hell do you think you are? You're a son of a bitch," the old man said, "that's what you are." He was wheezing.

"Daddy, hang up, please," the daughter said. "He's not been doing well. He's been very sick," she said, addressing me.

"I ain't sick. I'm fine," he said.

I heard one of the phones hang up and then I heard the daughter come into the room where the old man was.

"Daddy, give me the phone," I heard her say in the background.

There was some kind of struggle. I could hear some banging around. She was trying to get the phone from him.

"Leave me alone, get the hell off of me," I heard him say.

Then he addressed me again. "You little shit. Who the hell do you think you are?" he said.

"I'm sorry," I said right away, instinctively, but then I wasn't sure why I was apologizing. I snapped back at him. "Oh, well, I guess I should have let you die then," I said.

"You're damn right you should have," he said.

I heard the woman say *"Daddy!"* again and then the phone

clicked. It was quiet for a few seconds and then the dial tone came on. I sat there listening to its dull hum. I listened all the way through to the recording that tells you to hang up or try again. The loud beeps came on. I let them blare in my ear until they all ran together like the sound of someone flatlining.

Party

Eight or ten doctors ran past the waiting room and into the burn unit without scrubbing up. We, the family, looked on. We'd been waiting there for news.

"Where is it?" one doctor said.

"Bed Four," a nurse replied.

In a few minutes, the electric doors swung open and the medical personnel filed back out. One doctor who had heard the code blue from another wing was only just coming in. The other doctors were pulling the masks down from their faces and peeling off their latex gloves.

"They called off the dogs," one of them said, smiling. "No party here," he said.

Down Again

Alethea is dying, but we are sleeping together anyway.

"I'm like cancer, I spread quickly," she says.

I am going down on her again. It is the one thing I can give her in these last weeks of hers.

"I feel so alive," she screams.

I stay down on her until well after she is through. Then I come up, nestle my chin into her chest, and listen to her heart thump. It is a beautiful sound—the blood pumping to her cells in violent blights—and I wonder how long it will be until it stops. I wonder how many months, or weeks, she has. Later, while we have sex, I imagine our thrusts keeping time with her beating heart. I think, *I want to move in rhythm with her pumping blood, I want to feel the rest of her life.*

"Can I touch it?" I say when we are done.

"Not too hard," she says.

I touch the tips of my fingers to the scar on her neck. It's only four weeks since they took out the lump, so I touch it as tenderly as I can.

"It's so sexy," I say.

"You think?"

It turns me on in some way that I don't understand myself. I kiss her neck all around the scar and then I feel the crease where the stitches were with my tongue. The scar is rubbery and smooth.

"Yes, I do think so," I say.

When we're not having sex we're indulging in food. Last night we had pizza and champagne, "to celebrate her health," she said.

"I feel like something more involved tonight. I think I want to dine," she tells me.

She thumbs through the phone book looking for what she calls "a *suitable* place." I hear her make a reservation, but I don't know where it is. "Dress appropriately," she says when she hangs up the phone.

"How are we paying for this?" I whisper as the maître d' seats us at the restaurant. He's wearing a bow tie and a jacket with tails.

"I'm taking care of it," she says.

"How?"

"Mind your business," she tells me.

The waiter bows and interrupts and asks if he can bring us a cocktail while we decide. She orders for me.

"Two martinis. One wet, with an extra olive. And how do you want yours, Wilson?" she says, winking at me. While I deliberate, she smirks, purses her lips, and shakes her head patronizingly. "He'll have his dry," she says.

When the waiter leaves, she reaches across and pinches my cheek like I'm a child.

"You're not very clever, are you?" she says.

I just stare at her.

"Who do you think will pay my bills when I'm gone?" she says.

"Your insurance?"

"I don't have insurance."

"Your estate?"

"I don't own anything."

"I give up," I say. "Who?"

"No one, silly, I'll be dead." She reaches in her purse and produces three Visas, an American Express, and a MasterCard. She spreads them out in her fingers like a hand of cards.

"Great. I'll pick out the wine," I say.

For a first course, she orders quail on toast. She talks me into the wild boar pâté.

"I love game," she says. She spreads some of my pâté on her quail and then she breaks off the tiny drumstick and nibbles on the meat. "You can taste the life in it," she says.

For an entrée, she orders buffalo in a wild mushroom sauce. She tries to order for me again, but I insist on making my own choice this time. I get the flounder, poached in lemon and chardonnay.

"I'm in the mood for something light, okay?"

"Of course you are," she says.

When the waiter brings the wine and pours it for me to taste, she reaches across and snatches up my glass. She sips and nods approvingly and invites him to join us for a toast. He fills each of ours and pours himself a modest glass.

"To my body," she says.

"To your body," the waiter says, raising his glass, smiling slightly and looking generally confused.

When we are through with our entrées, she orders for me again.

"I'll have a cappuccino and so will he," she says. "How would you like yours, dear?" she asks. She leans over and touches the side of my face. "I'd like mine wet this time, I think. Yes, cappuccino wet for me," she says, smirking.

"And for you, sir?" the waiter says.

"Whatever," I say, feeling slightly embarrassed by her obsession with the texture of drinks, among other things.

The waiter smiles and shrugs at me.

"Dry, I guess," I say.

"And what about dessert for either of you?" he says.

"Do you have something with meat in it?" she asks.

This week she was in the hospital again. For this round of treatment, she took the radioactive pills instead of the standard chemotherapy. On the door there was a radioactive symbol with her name underneath. *DANGER: ALETHEA SHOPE,* it said. They wouldn't let me in to see her for three days, but they released her from the hospital today and now we're back in bed.

"Do you think I'm polluting you?" she asks.

"I hope so," I say.

She is dark-complected, olive-skinned, and I can see her skin is yellower, more pale, than it used to be. I can smell the radiation on her hair. It smells like chlorine.

"You should have seen it when they brought the pills in. The nurse had on three pairs of gloves. Three pairs!" she says.

I kiss her bottom lip and tuck what is left of her smooth black hair behind her ear.

" 'Try not to let the pills touch your skin,' the nurse said to me." She sits up and laughs and smiles at me. "I told her, 'Wait a minute, I can't touch them, but I'm supposed to eat the fucking things?' "

"And they're supposed to help you?" I say, smelling her hair, tucking it back again.

"What is that?" she says, laughing. "Can you imagine? I have to eat them, but I can't touch the goddamn things?"

She puts her hands on my hips and presses herself into me.

"I should tell you, the doctors said no relations for a week," she says.

"Really?"

"My fluids are glowing."

"I see."

"But doctors exaggerate, you know?"

"They're afraid of getting sued, I guess."

"You won't sue them, will you, sweetheart?" she says, caressing my stomach and hip.

"Of course I won't."

"I don't want to pollute you, though," she says.

"Pollute me, please," I tell her.

"Your insides will glow," she says.

They already are, I'm thinking, but before I can say it, she hugs me and rolls me on top of her and puts both her hands on my cheeks.

"Maybe we should run away," she says, touching her fingers to my lips.

I kiss her fingertips.

"Where do you want to go?" she asks.

"Anywhere," I say.

"Anywhere." She reaches between my legs. "Anywhere with you," she says.

. . .

She puts my fingers in her mouth and scooches up in bed and slides my face between her legs. She shivers and giggles and arches her back into my face.

"Will you, please?" she says.

I nod and smile and put her hand on the back of my head.

"Of course. Of course I will," I say, going down on her again.

Peaches

My friend Travis's parents had been stabbed and he wanted to spend the summer at the family farm where they had died. I moved in with him. One day I was relaxing on the living room couch when I heard him scream from the basement below. The police were to have cleaned up the murder scene, but some blood had seeped through the wooden floorboards and dripped into the cellar beneath. It stained the wooden pillars that ran up from the earth to support the home. It ran onto the jars of peaches his mother had canned the fall before.

Quantum Mechanics

Alethea's cancer was in remission, but we hadn't been getting along as well.

Moving to Idaho had been her idea—she wanted to try something new. We were in our rental trailer. She was making Kraft macaroni and cheese. I was eating deer bologna, drinking Pabst Blue Ribbon, watching TV.

"Darling, did you see this?" I said.

"See what?"

"This." She peeked out of the kitchen, which was really part of our living room. I pointed at the television. "This Stephen Hawking fella?" I said.

I don't usually use words like *darling* or *fella,* but I was feeling dark and high-toned, like late fall, I suppose.

"No, I don't know him," she said, tearing open the packet of powdered cheese.

I'm not sure of all of the reasons why I felt so compelled by Stephen Hawking at that moment. I do know that I, myself, am disposed to a kind of incurable restlessness. It cripples me regularly, leaves me helpless in the face of any task that requires my sitting in one place for more than just a few minutes. Stephen Hawking has amyotrophic lateral sclerosis, the motor neuron disease. He is unable to move or even speak. Yet from that position he has become one of the most prominent theoretical physicists of his day. *That* fascinates me.

"You don't know him?" I said.

She kept her back turned, kept stirring the macaroni.

"Do you want to know who he is?" I said.

She came into the living room and stared at the TV with the wooden stirring spoon in her hand.

"Is that him?"

"Yes, that's him," I said.

Some years before, I had read Stephen Hawking's book so I knew something about him. Among other things, I remembered the extraordinary fact of his having been born three hundred years to the day after Galileo's death.

"Listen. Listen to this," I said.

Hawking can only move his hand slightly, just enough to move a mouse and select words off a computer screen to structure his sentences. He speaks through a voice modulator. The computer does the talking.

"According to quantum mechanics, space is filled with virtual particles and anti-particles that are constantly materializing in pairs, separating, coming together again, and annihilating each other . . ."

If you're not familiar with the voice simulator, it can sound stilted and be difficult to understand. For some reason, at that moment, it felt crucial to me that she understand what he was saying.

"Did you hear that? Did you hear what he said?" I asked her.

"Yes, I heard it," she said.

"*Well?* What do you think?"

"He sounds like a bright guy," she said, and then she turned and walked back into the kitchen.

"He is, he is a bright guy. He's a very bright guy," I said.

I put another chunk of deer bologna in my mouth and watched her settle in at the stove. She rinsed her hands in the sink and then started stirring again.

"How's the macaroni coming?" I said.

She remained at the stove with her back turned.

"You staying on top of it?"

"What's that?" she said.

"The macaroni," I said again.

"Yes, I'm on top of it," she said, turning around and smiling pleasantly. "Thank you, though."

I should have known about Alethea by this time that if you pushed her too hard, you didn't get anywhere. In this case *Yes, I'm on top of it,* stated pleasantly, meant *You're acting strange, leave me the hell alone, thank you.*

"Do you want me to stir the macaroni while you watch Dr. Hawking?" I said.

"No, that's all right. I don't mind doing it," she told me.

I took a sip of my PBR, leaned back on the couch, and sighed. The show was back on and Hawking was talking through his voice modulator again.

"In the presence of a black hole, one member of a pair of virtual particles may fall into the hole, leaving the other member without a partner with which to annihilate . . ."

"Jesus, amazing," I said out loud.

She turned around at the stove and stared at me.

"I mean Jesus, Dr. Hawking, Jesus, this is fascinating," I said, pointing to the TV.

She turned down the stove, set the stirring spoon in the pot of macaroni, and came out into the living room. She took a seat in front of the TV, leaned forward with her elbows on her knees, and propped her chin on her fists. Her fists scrunched up her cheeks.

"Scientific theories assume we are rational beings who are free to observe the universe as we want and to draw logical deductions from what we see. Yet if there really is a complete unified theory, it would also presumably determine our actions. And so the theory itself could determine the outcome of our search for it! Why should it determine that we come to the right conclusions from the evidence? Might it not equally well determine that we draw the wrong conclusion? Or no conclusion at all?"

I muted the TV and looked at her.

"Did you hear that?" I said.

"I heard it," she said.

She raised her thin black eyebrows in a way that seemed, to me, physically impossible. They turned in and downward in the middle at a near right angle, like a cartoon character's.

"How often do you hear a scientist wrestling with those kinds of questions?"

"It's interesting," she said.

"You think so?" I asked her.

"I do," she said.

Alethea. "Not false," in the Greek, literally translated.

"What's interesting about it, then?" I said.

She let her eyebrows fall and stared at the TV. I watched her patiently, waiting for an answer, but she just kept staring at the screen. The television was still muted. After five or ten seconds of silence, I finally raised *my* eyebrows, shook *my* head, and said, "*Well?*"

She stared back at me, smiled mildly and calmly, and said, "I'm sorry, what, dear?"

What is it in the constitution of the human animal that drives them to, say, put all their money on a single number at a roulette wheel, or wager their entire paycheck on one roll of the dice? Is it related, simply, to the under- or overproduction of certain chemicals in our brains at a given moment? The effective or ineffective functioning of neurotransmitters? Recently, while filling a prescription, I read a pamphlet from off of the pharmacist's desk about the relationship of food to brain functioning. High-fat foods—like cheese, for example—divert blood away from the brain and dull cognitive processes. Lean proteins, on the other hand—like deer bologna—provide the protein that brain tissue needs without sacrificing digestive efficiency. Is that what's at work in cases like this, where you decide to take an irrational risk? Where you whimsically try to make progress with someone even though you know it's nearly impossible? Or is there some kind of logic, however skewed, to the decision to take such a gamble?

"This wouldn't be one of those times where you're *indulging* me, is it?" I asked her.

"I told you, I'm interested," she said flatly.

Occasionally, during this time, Alethea would come home with one of those nauseating glamour magazines. You know the ones: *Marie Claire, Cosmopolitan, Glamour Girl,* whatever they are. She knew it annoyed me and, truthfully, I think she did it for just that reason. When I would address the issue, she'd say something like, "I'm stuck here in Idaho, I need to know how to look good, at least." She'd do things like drive an hour and fifteen minutes to Boise and pay eighty dollars for pants, and then, a week later, drive back and return them because, she'd say, they didn't look right on her hips.

"I see. I can see that you're interested," I said.

"Thank you. Thank you very much," she said.

As she thanked me, she let her long dark hair fall in front of her face and she began filtering the ends through her fingertips. Before she found out she had cancer, she had never cared about her appearance. But after her radiation therapy, she became obsessed with hair. She was always searching for damaged, split ends.

"Most scientists aren't complicated enough to consider existential questions," I said, pushing my luck again.

She looked up, but held on to her hair. "He's a scientist," she said.

"He's a theoretical physicist," I said.

She blinked and nodded at me. "And what is that, exactly?"

"It means he's concerned with more than just hard science," I said. "He's concerned with origins, with questions of meaning."

There was a situation that emerged with my ex-wife and I leading up to our final separation when I became somewhat focused on a roach problem we had. I got consumed with them, felt that they had a kind of poetic or philosophical power over our relationship. I'll admit I have a kind of a problem, that I can become very emphatic in a discussion of the metaphorical, even metaphysical, implications of certain events and objects, but let me take the liberty here to explain a few things. Let me say that I just don't comprehend the superficiality of our culture. Obviously, I can't stand those glamour magazines, but a kind of superficiality has even infiltrated the academy. For thousands of years it was all anyone was concerned with: the nature of God, God's existence or nonexistence, questions of meaning. From Plato to Kierkegaard, it was all philosophers talked about. Now a few clever thinkers come along in the late twentieth century and suddenly it's out of vogue to even think about such things. I'm not saying that you have to end up believing a certain set of axioms about God or that a certain set of beliefs are the right ones. I'm not even saying that there is a God. I just think that it's absurd to deny the impulse to inquire into such things. The impulse to look beyond oneself, to consider the source or meaning of existence, is nearly as old and natural as the urge to procreate.

"I thought he's a *physicist,*" she said.

She let her dark hair fall in front of her face again and resumed her search for split ends. "He is a physicist," I said, "but he's a *theoretical* physicist. He's interested in the bigger, more profound questions."

"More *profound* ones?"

"That's what I'd call them," I said.

She nodded, disinterested.

"Why is he in the wheelchair?" she said.

"He has something called ALS. Amyotrophic lateral sclerosis, the motor neuron disease. He's been practically an invalid since his late twenties," I said.

I turned the volume back up on the TV. Dr. Hawking was speaking again.

"What do we know about the universe and how do we know it?" Once again, the voice simulator was making it difficult to understand, so I turned the volume up some more. *"Where did the universe come from, and where is it going? Did the universe have a beginning, and if so, what happened before then?"*

How refreshing, I thought, *a scientist willing to consider philosophical, even theological questions.*

"Do you see?" I said.

She nodded unconvincingly.

"What? What do you see?" I said.

She held her ground, not speaking.

"He's asking all of *the* questions."

"All of *what* questions?"

"All of *the* questions," I said.

I took another bite of deer bologna, stared at her as I chewed.

"Would you like some cheese with that?" she said, smirking. She was diverting the conversation, staving off the threat of philosophical substance.

"With what?"

"With the bologna," she said.

"No, thanks, I don't want to dull brain functioning," I said, remembering the pamphlet from the doctor's office.

She shook her head and formed a near right angle with her black eyebrows again.

"What are you talking about?" she said.

"Venison is brain food," I said.

"Okay?" she said, craning her neck forward.

"Cheese diverts blood away from the brain."

"*What?*" she said, shaking her head, flopping her hair back and forth in front of her face.

"Nothing. Never mind," I said, putting my finger to my lips to signal that Hawking was speaking again.

I pointed to the TV and then I studied her reaction while she watched. She pursed her lips. They were full and curled down at the edges. They fell that way naturally, when she wasn't smiling. It made her look pensive, philosophical—appealing.

"*Ever since the dawn of civilization, people have not been content to see events as unconnected and inexplicable. Today we still yearn to know why we are here and where we came from. Humanity's deepest desire for knowledge is justification enough for our continuing quest. What is the nature of time? Will it ever come to an end? Where did the universe come from? How and why did it begin?"* Dr. Hawking said.

She came over and snuggled up next to me on the couch. She stroked my forehead with one hand and she slid her other hand down my arm. She took the remote from me and clicked off the television.

"You know how I hate TV," she said.

It's true, she did hate TV. I hated it, too. I still do. I hate how it entertains, because that's all it does, *entertain*. I hate its superficiality, the simple clichés that go as epiphanies. But for some reason, this Hawking spot was an exception for me.

"I hate TV, too," I said.

"I know you do," she said, stroking my forehead. "Let's eat my macaroni and cheese."

"Okay, let's do," I said, acquiescing.

She pecked me on the cheek and we got up off the couch and embraced for a few moments before we walked to the dinner table. I poured the water and put out the plates, napkins, and cutlery because, on this night, she had made the food. We broke pieces off a loaf of half-eaten French bread and split up what remained of some cheap Merlot from the previous evening. I carried the plate of bologna from the living room so I could eat little pieces alongside the macaroni and bread. I offered her a few venison chunks, but she declined.

"I thought you like game," I said.

"That was when I was dying—on my meat kick—sucking the marrow out of life," she said.

"Suck some marrow out of this. It's high-grade bologna. It's venison, very lean, very high quality."

She nodded and pretended to smile.

"No thanks," she said.

After a few minutes, I got up to refill my water glass and I noticed one of her *Marie Claire* magazines on the counter, next to the stove. When I sat back down, I gestured to it with a raise of my chin and took a bite of macaroni. I chewed with my mouth full.

"Why do you read those things?" I said.

"I don't actually read them."

"What do you do to them, then?" I said.

"I look at them."

"Why do you look at them?"

"For fun."

"Fun?"

"Yes, *fun*," she said.

I took a sip of wine and said, "You like *Marie Claire,* but you don't like TV?"

"That's right," she said, taking a sip of her own wine and peering back at me. "I like the pretty pictures." She smiled blankly, sarcastically.

When we were very near the end of dinner and when it was appropriate I said, "Do you mind if I do the dishes later? I'd like to go for a walk by myself."

She said, "No, of course I don't mind," in a way that meant, *Yes I do mind, but I'm not going to stop you.*

I put on my jacket and went out of the house.

The street was empty and quiet except for the sound of some dogs barking back and forth at one another. The temperature had dropped twenty degrees since I had come home from the local hardware store, where I had taken a job a few weeks before. It was well below zero and I felt my nose hairs freezing with each breath. I had no business being out without a hat or gloves, but I walked in the direction of the post office and the two or three businesses that were next door to it anyway.

There was no sidewalk. I was walking on the side of the road, on the frozen dirt. Every couple of hundred feet there was a small house or house trailer, and I could see light from the TVs inside the houses blinking on the walls. Each time I passed in front of a residence, walked on the edge of the dying grass on the lawns, I had the feeling that I was intruding on their lives. The frozen dirt and grass made an obvious cracking sound under my boots, as if I was crunching large insects. I could still hear the dogs barking and it seemed like they were exposing me, yelping at their owners, alerting their masters to my presence, like I was a rabbit or bird to be hunted. Trespassing isn't looked on favorably in Idaho. For some of the crankier, more reclusive residents, *trespassing* consists merely of walking on the edge of a property line, an infraction that poses an obvious threat, enforceable with force—likely firearms— by the landowner. A couple of times I thought I heard footsteps behind me. Once I thought I saw a shadow fall over my back and I wheeled around to see what was there. I had imagined it, of course.

When I finally got downtown, or what you might call downtown, I noticed the lights on in the quaint little library next to the municipal building. My ears and nose and fingers were numb from the cold—probably almost frostbitten—so I decided to go in and get warm. I nodded at the polite librarian as I went past the front desk. She had been friendly and kind to me the other times I'd been in—friendly and kind, but not overly talkative, which I appreciated. The library was small and didn't get much use, so she was pleased with anyone who showed interest.

It was only two rooms. Along one of the walls, to the right of an old, retired wooden card catalog, were shelves of home videos. I thought of looking for a novel to sign out, but I was afraid I'd be too restless to read for the remainder of the evening, so I scanned the home videos.

It's true that part of what you lack in Idaho is entertaining things. You lack distractions: places to shop, restaurants, bars, even neon signs. You would think that without these things your life would take on more depth, more meaning. But it doesn't always work that way. You're surrounded by all of these wonderful, natural, aesthetic vistas, mountains, rivers, herds of sheep, buffalo on the plains, but you've got no one with whom to reflect on that beauty.

"Can I help you find something?" she said.

The place was so small that it wasn't even organized with Dewey decimals. There were just categories of books arranged alphabetically.

"Is there a science section?" I asked.

"The science is right here," she said. "Anything in particular?"

"Theoretical physics," I said.

"You mean like . . . astronomy?"

"I mean like . . . *theoretical physics,* like . . . *why are we here?*" I felt bad immediately. I had probably sounded abrupt, patronizing. She looked puzzled. Likely, aside from my being rude, she thought I was strange or mysterious for wanting a book on such a topic. I wondered about her like you do about librarians. What do they like to read? Are they actually thoughtful and intelligent, or are they just diligent organizers?

"I guess you'll just have to look through them," she said. "These two shelves are all science," she said.

"Thank you very much," I said.

I scanned through them and opened and looked at a few. They looked very complicated. They drew their arguments from logarithmic equations and incomprehensible diagrams.

"What exactly are you looking for?" she said.

"I'm not sure, actually," I said.

At that, though, she left me alone and I browsed for a couple of minutes in silence. The science was arranged alphabetically—there weren't more than thirty science titles—and I scanned immediately ahead to the *H*s. No Stephen Hawking.

"Damn," I mumbled too loudly.

The librarian looked up from her desk—from whatever it was that she was scribbling, organizing—and took off her glasses.

"We're closing soon. At eight o'clock." She studied me. "That's in ten minutes," she said.

She watched me some more, with her glasses back on, and then she said, "If there is a particular title, I can direct you to it . . . it might . . . simplify . . . expedite things."

"I'm looking for a book by Stephen Hawking," I said.

"Oh, Stephen Hawking. It's over there, with the popular books."

"Popular books?"

"It's very popular, a bestseller," she said.

I felt momentarily critical of myself, called into question my own taste. But I wanted it anyway.

"Where is it?" I asked.

"I can see it from here." She lifted her chin, trying to direct me. "Over there. Next to King, the horror writer. You must know him. Next to *K*," she said. She pushed out her chair and walked, pointing, to a set of shelves opposite her desk. "Here," she said, pulling the Hawking book halfway out so it was distinguishable from the others. "Anything else?"

"No, nothing else," I said, signing out the book.

It seemed even colder and more ominous on the walk home than it had on the way. I felt unsafe, even more unsafe than I had before. I tried to force myself not to yield to my own paranoia. A number of times when I thought I heard sounds, I refused myself the luxury of a look behind.

It's strange with me, how things flood out of my past into my conscious memory at unpredictable times. At this moment, walking—irrationally afraid of what was behind me—what I thought of was a very good friend of mine whose parents, years before, were murdered. I'm not sure if it was the philosophical musings that made me think of it or if it was just the sense that I was in physical danger, being stalked by something unseen. I thought of my friend and then I thought of his parents, whom I knew only as acquaintances. I imagined what they were doing, how they were feeling in the moments before the intruder snuck in. The father was a psychiatrist and it was one of his patients—sick, lonely, misfiring—who committed the crime. My friend's father was probably reading a journal, perhaps a literary magazine, smoking the pipe he smoked evenings, when the patient snuck in and stabbed him. The mother was probably making tea, perhaps baking. She heard the commotion, came running in, was stabbed, and bled to death next to her husband. My orphaned friend told me these things about his parents' final moments as he showed me the house, the house of his youth, on a return visit to it we took the summer after the murders. We found bloodstains on the floorboards, in the basement.

I glanced in at one of the house trailers as I walked on the edge of its property. There was, of all things, a ski boat in the driveway with an old Mercury 150 mounted on the back. The fishing lodge

I had worked for on a small Caribbean island a few years before had used Mercury engines. I tried to remember what it was like to feel like I had felt during that time of my life. Safe, warm, free, and unaffected. I wondered about the people in the trailer. Somebody had had a dream of sun and water. A dream of warmth, safety, freedom. Now, for the two months a year that it was over seventy degrees in Idaho, and for the cost of a year's income, they got to run their boat around in a reservoir—that is, if the engine happened to be functioning.

I came upon our rental trailer and entered through the side door carrying Stephen Hawking's *A Brief History of Time,* my would-be antidote for this Idaho evening's tedium. I had envisioned myself indulging in it, over scotch, until I grew drowsy and was able to doze off peacefully. But the house trailer was too quiet, too full of entropy.

Alethea didn't come out to greet me, but I could feel her presence, her tense breathing, in another part of the trailer. The TV was off. I sat down on the couch and opened my new book.

She came into the kitchen and went to the counter holding an empty beer bottle. She put it under the sink in our recycling bin and got a fresh one out of the refrigerator. I watched her twist off the cap and waited for her to look up at me. She didn't. Instead, she picked up *Mademoiselle* and headed for the bedroom.

"How's it going?" I said.

She stopped abruptly, apparently startled by my presence.

"Fine," she said. "It's going fine."

"Good," I said.

"Did you have a nice walk?" she asked.

"Sure," I told her.

She took a sip of her Pabst and paused in the doorway to the bedroom.

"I picked up this book," I said, holding it up for her to see.

"What is it?"

"Stephen Hawking."

"Oh," she said, nodding awkwardly.

There was a period of silence during which she appeared to be considering something very carefully.

"Going to read the magazine?"

"Yeah, to look at it," she said.

She wiped some condensation off the beer bottle and examined the moisture it left on her fingertips.

"Do you know what entropy is?" I said.

"No, I don't," she said, stiffening.

"Do you want to know?"

She shrugged and said, "Not particularly, no, I don't."

I suppose, from my end, it had something to do with remote places, with what I was saying before about nature. From her end, I think, it had something to do with her disease. Musing philosophically about life or death forced her, against her will, to face her life-or-death issues.

"You know, Wilson—" she said.

"I just think this stuff is interesting," I interrupted.

She was leaning in the doorway, looking spent, resting her head.

"Don't you want to know about entropy?" I said.

"What about it?"

"Don't you want to know what it is?"

She sighed and crossed her arms.

"Okay, what is entropy?" she said, raising both eyebrows.

"Entropy is the measure of disorder in a given system," I said.

She shook her head, not comprehending. "Okay . . . ?" she said.

"If you put two particles together, entropy increases," I said.

She rubbed her forehead.

"Okay, here's what I'm trying to say," I said.

"*What?* What *are you* trying to say?" she said.

"I think that things of consequence happen . . . and then you have to ask yourself, *why?* You ask yourself, '*Why? Why* did it happen?' If something random and tragic befalls you, you start grappling, you start asking metaphysical, even theological questions, without realizing it. You think, 'Did this happen for a reason? *Do* things happen for reasons? How could it have happened in a decent world? Is the world all gone to hell? Is the world entropic? Is it all just random?' " I paused for effect. "Do you know what I'm talking about?" I said.

She fondled her split ends, denied me eye contact.

"They're natural questions, healthy grapplings," I said. "Don't you think?"

She kept fondling her hair. I waited for an answer.

"Don't you think? Don't you think they're healthy questions?"

She stared at the floor for five or ten seconds and then she looked up at me and said, "Are you through . . . with this?"

Of course I was offended, so I felt justified in pushing it further.

"Well, are you?" I said.

"Am I what?" she said.

"Are you grappling?"

She turned around abruptly to go into the bedroom, and as she did, her beer slipped out of her hand. It landed on its side and started pouring out on the linoleum.

"Goddamn it," she said.

She picked it up, stomped over to the sink, and held it there until it quit foaming.

"Why are you so angry?" I said.

"I'm not angry."

"You look angry."

"I'm *not angry,* I just spilled my beer, okay?" she said.

She came back into the living room, tossed a dishrag on the puddle of beer, and massaged it under her foot, aggressively.

"Why don't you just admit it when you're angry?" I said.

She got down on her hands and knees and wiped at the floor. She flopped the rag over and sopped up some more beer with the other side.

"Why don't you let me admit what I want to admit?"

I waited, but she just kept scrubbing, refused to respond. She carried the beer-sodden rag to the sink, wrung it out, rinsed her hands, and headed for the bedroom. I tried to follow her in, but she slammed the door in my face.

"Do you see what I'm saying?" I said, talking through the door. "You don't grapple and then you start banging around, slamming doors."

"I know, I don't grapple," she said.

I stayed by the door, waiting.

"And I'm the problem," she said.

"I didn't say that."

"Look, why don't you just leave me alone for a while?" I could hear that she had walked to the far side of the bedroom. I had my ear pressed against the door. "I wish you'd just leave me alone . . . *just fucking leave me alone!*" she screamed.

I was hurt, irrational. "Do you *ever* think about the fact that you have a fucking life-threatening disease?" I said, before I could stop myself.

There was no response on the other side of the door.

I got a beer out of the refrigerator and went over and sat down on the couch. I heard the springs creek as Alethea lay down on the bed in the bedroom. I looked around the quiet, empty room, stared at the blank TV screen, saw the VCR clock blinking 12:00

at me. I thought about trying to read, but I was certain that now I wouldn't be able to without getting restless. I saw the remote on the floor in front of the couch and I went over and clicked on the TV. Amazingly, the Hawking documentary was still on. It was just ending. The camera was zooming in on his face. He was giving his final words, final insights. His head was tilted sideways, supported by a brace on the back of his wheelchair and his bottom lip was protruding. It looked like saliva was about to dribble out of his mouth. His eyes were bulgy, vacuous.

"Einstein said, 'God does not play dice.' But it appears that Einstein was doubly wrong," he said.

In the background, under the eerie sound of Hawking's voice simulator, I could hear Alethea's soft, rhythmic sobs.

"The quantum effects of black holes suggest that not only does God play dice, he sometimes throws them where they cannot be seen."

The credits started flashing up, and I clicked off the TV. I sat there in silence, staring at the blank screen, wondering what I was going to do next.

I considered going and knocking on the door, trying to get her to let me in, but that wasn't going to happen. I put on my jacket, hat, and gloves and stepped out the back door into our dirt yard.

In that moment, as I stood there in the dirt yard behind our trailer, I saw something that I'd never seen before, something that I know I may never see again. I saw, in the field behind our trailer, just next to the woods, a coyote stalking a hare. Now hares are very good runners and they are rather large, almost too large, I would have thought, for a coyote to target. And coyotes, I had thought, were primarily scavengers, so at the time I thought it a bit strange to see this animal hunting. I've since learned that coyotes also hunt and kill for much of their diet. This animal certainly planned to. He was sneaking up on the hare, *stalking* it.

To get a better view, I tiptoed to the back edge of our yard. The coyote was closing in, furtively. He was about to pounce.

In the next moment, I did something that surprised even me, something that I hadn't known I would do until I was doing it. I took off running, straight at the coyote.

"Leave it alone," I shouted.

The hare bolted first. It got away.

The coyote turned toward me and crouched. I stopped running and crouched also. For a moment, we stood there locked in a kind of a staring match.

Coyotes aren't that big and I'd never heard of one turning and attacking a human, but any creature will attack when it feels cornered or threatened. This coyote must have felt threatened. It couldn't have been pleased with me. It had ways of surviving the cold Idaho winter. I had interfered.

I was ready, poised for it to make a move in my direction. But it didn't. It turned and headed into the dark woods, out of my view.

Barbecue

It was the first Mother's Day after Travis's parents had been stabbed. We decided to stay at his parents' farm to have a barbecue and look at slides. I volunteered to grill the meat.

There was a set of knives that hung in sheaths, in a rack, by the kitchen sink. When I went to trim the fat off the steaks, I noticed one was gone.

Afterwards, Rudy was washing the dishes and I was carrying them in to him from the picnic table on the porch, outside.

"Are all the dishes in now?" Rudy said, hanging up the knives.

Travis came into the kitchen and opened the refrigerator

door. We waited until he'd taken out a beer and opened it. We waited until he'd gone back outside.

"Is there another knife for here?" Rudy said, after Travis had gone.

"No, there isn't. The dishes are all in. The set was missing one," I said.

Searching for Intruders

This was while Alethea's cancer was taking over again, but before we realized it. We had been getting along well again, renting a house back in Reading.

There was a heat wave and we had no air conditioner. It was late, almost 2:00 A.M. We were naked in bed. She was caressing me and we were about to make love when we heard the screams.

"What was that?" she said, stiffening.

"I don't know," I said, sitting up myself.

I crawled out of bed and tiptoed across the room, naked, to turn off the fan, which was oscillating and whirring. I switched it off and sat back down on the bed at Alethea's feet. She had pulled the sheet up over her breasts.

"Whatever it was, I didn't like it," she said. She looked pale, terrified.

"*Shh.* Listen," I said, putting my fingers up to my lips.

We heard it again, or thought we heard it. It was so faint that it was hard to be certain. It was a kind of a high-pitched squeal followed by what sounded like it might have been a human voice saying, *No!*

"Did you hear it that time?" she said.

"I think so."

"What was it?"

"I don't know," I said.

I was still naked. I stood up at the foot of the bed and pushed the window up higher than it already was. I put up the screen and stuck my head out. I listened for ten or fifteen seconds, but I didn't hear anything else. I sat back down at the foot of the bed and looked back at Alethea. She was still sitting up in the same position, with her beautiful long, dark, but thinning hair spilling down onto the sheets she had wrapped around her body and chest.

"It might not be anything. It's probably some drunk people coming out of the golf course clubhouse," I said.

She pulled her knees up to her chest and locked her hands in front of her shins.

"Wait, there it was again," she said, dropping the sheet, sliding up to the end of the bed next to me. She covered her chest with her arms and peeked out the window. "Didn't you hear it?" she said.

"I think I heard it," I said.

"What was it?"

"I don't know."

"It sounded almost . . . inhuman," she said.

"It sounded like a dying rabbit," I said.

"Like what?"

"Like a dying rabbit. Rabbits squeal like that when they're dying. They sort of scream," I said.

Just as I finished talking, the sound came again. A faint, barely audible, high-pitched moan.

"That doesn't sound like a rabbit," she said.

"No, probably not."

I dug around and found my boxer shorts balled up in the sheets at the foot of the bed. I got out of bed and put them on.

"Where are you going?" she said.

"I don't know."

I went out of the bedroom and flipped the light on at the top of the steps. I went downstairs into the kitchen and out through the back door onto the porch. I was barefoot and I wasn't wearing a shirt, so I felt a bit naked, a bit exposed, but I didn't feel like going back in and looking for clothing. The porch light was on. I reached inside the door and turned it off and then came back out and stood on the edge of the porch. I listened for a while from there and then I walked out into our yard and listened some more. I bent down, squinting, trying to get a clear view through the trees. I knew there was a set of tennis courts beyond them and, on the other side of the courts, the eighteenth green. For some reason, though I couldn't even see the green, I pictured a man and a woman there. I imagined the woman pinned in the sand trap, screaming for help. I held my breath for a few seconds, staring through the trees, listening.

I heard a noise behind me and I wheeled around. It was Alethea. She was standing on the back porch with her arms folded. She had put on a long shirt that came all the way down over her hips like a dress. I looked back into the trees and then off at the neighbor's farm to the right. The lights were on in the house. I listened and looked for silhouettes moving inside, but once again, I couldn't see or hear anything.

I walked all the way back to the edge of the yard where the woods began. I took a few steps into them, but I didn't have any shoes on. I stopped and listened a little more and then I turned and walked back to the porch. Alethea had stepped back inside the storm door. She moved to the side as I stepped in.

"Well?" she said.

I shrugged.

"You didn't see anything?" she said.

"No, I didn't."

We stood there staring out through the storm door window into the trees.

"I guess that doesn't mean there's no one out there," she said after a few moments.

"I guess not."

I shut the main door and bolted it.

"Well, what are we going to do?"

"What do you think we should do?"

"I don't know."

"I don't know either," I said.

I drew myself a glass of water and drank it straight down while she stared at me. I wiped the sweat off my forehead and poured another glass for myself.

"Water?" I asked.

"I'm not thirsty," she said.

"Are you sure?" I said, drinking some more down.

"I'm sure."

"You're probably dehydrated," I said, refilling my glass.

"I don't care if I am," she said.

We stood there in silence for five or ten seconds. She stared out through the window in the door. I drank some more, making loud gulping sounds without meaning to.

"Well, should we go back to bed?" I said, exhaling after my last swig.

She was still staring outside with her arms crossed. "I guess," she said, without looking at me.

The lights were still on in the kitchen. I turned them off and went over and stood next to Alethea. I stared out through the window and gazed into the dark trees, like she was.

"You see anything out there?" I said.

"No, nothing."

I stood there with her for what must have been nearly a minute.

"Well, I'm going to go upstairs now," I said, watching her. She kept staring out into the dark. I turned around and headed across the kitchen for the steps.

"I'll be up after a bit," she said.

When I got up to the bedroom, I turned the fan back on and I scooted the dresser it was resting on a couple of feet closer to the bed. I made sure the fan was aimed in such a way that the air would be coming over us, cooling us, as we slept. I stood in front of it and let the air blow on my face for a while and then I climbed back into bed. I left my boxer shorts on this time. I lay on my back, interlocked my hands behind my neck, and stared at the ceiling, listening. I had planned to wait there like that until Alethea came up and got back into bed with me, but the whir of the fan had a hypnotizing effect. I fell asleep.

After a while, I flinched awake, aware of something, though I wasn't sure what. I didn't know how long I'd been sleeping. I was in bed alone. Alethea still hadn't come up.

I got out of bed and turned off the fan.

"Alethea? Are you down there?" I said softly.

I went back downstairs into the kitchen and I called for her again.

"Alethea? Are you in here?" I said.

I looked in the living room thinking maybe she'd lain down on the couch and fallen asleep, but she wasn't there. I called down into the basement and waited, listening, but there was no response there either. I came back into the kitchen and looked outside through the back door. The porch light and the light attached to the side of the garage were on. The back door was unlocked. I put on some sneakers, stepped out onto the porch, and called for her again.

"Alethea?" I didn't know whether to shout or to whisper. "Are you out there?" I said.

I walked into the back yard and looked off toward the neighbors' where the lights had been on, but they were off now. I looked to the left of the house where, a couple of hundred yards away, there were more houses and, past them, more wooded areas. The porch light and the floodlight on the garage were pouring light into the back yard. I walked to the back edge of the yard to the wooded area and peered in. The lights from the house were shining on the near side of the tree trunks and the trees were casting shadows on the ground. Where the light from the house ended, it was very dark, very difficult to see. I realized again that I was practically naked. I was wearing only my boxer shorts and sneakers, but I walked back into the woods anyway. I walked back in as far as the light from the house reached, and stared back into the dark. I could just see the outline of the tennis courts on the other side.

"Alethea, are you out there?" I said out loud, in a normal voice. "Alethea?" I said a little louder, almost shouting, but there was still nothing.

I went ahead and walked the rest of the way through the trees and came out at the edge of the tennis courts. They were nice clay courts with fancy, low fences. I gazed out across them, staring at the perfect white stripes that marked the boundaries. I noticed two sets of footprints in the tidily swept clay going toward the baseline on the right side of the court. I followed them. Both sets of tracks stopped at the back fence, in the corner. The clay was smeared in that area as if someone had shuffled around or lain out on the ground. I stared at the smeared-out area for a few moments and then looked at how the tracks started again. Both sets started. I got down on my knees and looked. The one set of footprints was considerably larger than the other. In a few places, the big print was planted on top, covering, even wiping out the smaller footprint. The bigger one was, I figured, about a size thirteen. The other print looked like a woman's or child's size. I examined the smaller one, trying to remember what size Alethea wore, but there was no way to tell if it was hers. I didn't know what the bottom of her shoes looked like. I didn't even know if she had put shoes on.

I followed the tracks back up to the net and onto the neighboring court. They went straight across the other court and out the other side onto the grass, where I could no longer track them. I walked past a small building that was apparently the tennis pro shop and across a patio to the next set of courts. I stood and looked over the gate, but there were no tracks there, no sign that anyone had been through.

I walked along the outside of the last set of courts. I stopped on the far side of them. I looked in toward the golf clubhouse parking lot. There were a few outdoor lights on the building and there was light from the swimming pool illuminating part of the lot— enough to show just a silhouette of a person if there had been someone. But there was nothing there, not as far as I could tell.

I walked past the last tennis court through another set of trees until I came up on the eighteenth green. I stood there for a moment looking around. There was no wind. The pin was in, jutting up out of the cup in the center of the green, but the flag hung limp from the top of it. I walked over to the pin and took it out and then I jammed it back in the hole again. I walked over to one of the sand traps and peered down over the edge. It was a very deep bunker. It dipped down well below ground level in the belly—so low that if you sat or lay in it, no one would be able to see you unless they walked right up to the edge. In fact, someone had been lying in it. There was a wooden ladder that led down into the trap and there were footprints that started at the base of the ladder. They led over to the deepest section in the corner near the tennis courts and then the sand was smeared—smeared in much the same way that the area in the clay courts had been—as if some-one had lain down there for some reason. The sand was even dug out a bit. It looked like someone had wanted to make the sand trap deeper than it already was—perhaps to conceal whatever it was they were up to.

I looked up the fairway for Alethea, or for anything, but it was very dark in that direction. I scanned the parking lot near the golf clubhouse again, but I didn't see anything. I looked back toward the tennis courts, toward the tennis pro shop. There I did see something. I saw it just out of the corner of my eye: a black silhou-ette moving quickly between the courts, moving across and behind the building. Without taking time to think through what I was doing, I dropped to the ground and rolled down into the sand trap. The steep lip sent me tumbling down into the belly of it. I came to rest on my back and I lay for a moment breathing heavily, trying to figure out what to do. I didn't know where Alethea was. If she was outside somewhere, where this other figure was lurking, she could be in great danger. But she could also be in danger if she had fled back into the house. Maybe this guy had seen her go back in. Maybe now he was moving in toward the house. Maybe now he was stalking *her*.

I crawled on my stomach, on my elbows, up to the edge of the bunker and I lifted my head slowly to look out over the lip. I saw it clearly this time: the same silhouette. It came out from behind the building and moved across the tennis court where I had seen the tracks earlier. It scampered across, hunching down almost to the level of the net.

When the figure went off the far side of the court, it disappeared into the darkness of the trees. It seemed to be heading in toward the back porch.

I lay there for a few moments, panicking. Suddenly I felt unsure whether Alethea had ever left the house. Maybe I hadn't checked it carefully enough. I remembered that I had never checked the upstairs bathroom—the most obvious place. And I had been calling very softly when I was looking for her, almost whispering. Maybe she hadn't heard me. Maybe she had gone into the bathroom to take a bath, which she often did, and fallen asleep there. Maybe she'd even fainted.

Whatever the case, I felt certain she was in the house. And now this other figure was headed through the woods toward the back door.

I climbed out of the bunker and shuffled through the cluster of trees that separated the green and the first set of tennis courts. I hid behind a couple of small shrubs next to the court, catching my breath, and then ran up to the tennis pro shop. I peeked around the edge of the building and searched for movement in the illuminated section of the trees on the far side, near the house, but I didn't see anything. I had seen the figure disappear into the woods, but I hadn't seen where it had gone after that. It wasn't very appealing, the idea of having to head into the dark trees where I could be waylaid, but it was the shortest way in and now I felt like I had to get back there fast—like Alethea's life depended on it. The only thing for me to do was to make a run for it all the way to the back porch. I certainly wasn't going to sneak through the trees slowly, and make myself an easy target for something I couldn't see. If he was going to take me out, he was going to have to take me out running.

That is what I did. I ran. I sprinted. Once I tripped on a log, on a small tree that was lying horizontal on the ground. My shin slammed into it and I landed on my face in the moist dirt, but I hopped back to my feet, my adrenaline pumping, and started running again. I sprinted, utterly believing that something hiding in the dark had set the log there and that whatever had set it there was about to pounce on me. I sprinted on through the dark section of woods. As I came into the light from the house I felt some relief, like I was almost in the clear, but as I came out of the trees into the lawn, the floodlight on the garage and the porch light flicked off and right after that, the kitchen and living room lights went out. Now, as I sprinted, I had a decision to make. I could keep running straight for the back porch door where I had been planning to enter, or I could veer off behind the garage and figure out what to do next. Why had the lights gone off? Was the figure already inside, stalking Alethea? Had he come into the basement and flipped the breaker? Had he seen me running? Had he turned the lights off from right there in the kitchen, right by the back porch door? I had to process all of this in just one or two seconds, running at full tilt.

I veered off. I stood with my back to the garage, trying not to breathe so heavily that I'd be heard. Now I felt I had to *sneak* into the house. Alethea might be inside—or she might not—but this intruder was in there now, I was certain of that.

I figured he must have seen me or he wouldn't have turned off the light. But now I was also wondering: *Why had he turned out the light?* With it on, after all, he could see me, he could see where I was outside the house. Was it because I wasn't his target? Was it because it was only Alethea he wanted? Was he *more* concerned with concealing himself, with concealing whatever it was he was doing, than with capturing me? Did he figure, from inside the dark house, that he'd be able to see me, but not me him? I came to a kind of split-second conclusion that seemed to me, in that moment, profoundly significant: I decided that for this figure, remaining in the dark where he couldn't be seen was more important even than getting whatever it was he was after.

What I wasn't going to do was walk right into the house. I tried to remember what windows were open or unlocked. There was the laundry window on the far side of the garage, but if this guy had any intelligence, that was the first place he would look for me to come in. It was the first window on the other side of the garage and he had seen me veer off in that direction. I couldn't go around the house the other way because I'd have to go right by the porch, in plain view. Just inside there were the light switches for the lights he'd flipped off when I'd come running out of the woods. He might still be standing there, watching for me.

Whatever I was going to do, I needed to do it quickly.

I made another split-second decision. There were a few folding chairs propped up by our little hibachi, by the garage. I set one up as quickly and quietly as I could right next to the garage wall and I stepped up on it and grabbed onto the roof. Normally I strain just to do a couple of pull-ups, but at that moment, with my adrenaline pumping, I was able to yank myself up silently and easily. As soon as I was up, I had the presence of mind to take my shoes off so my steps would be more difficult to hear inside the house. I tiptoed over to where the roof gabled up to the main part of the house and I hoisted myself up onto the next level. I looked behind me for a moment, leaning on the chimney. I could see the tennis courts through the trees and I could see the parking lot in front of the golf course. I scanned everything hoping I'd see Alethea, but I didn't. I felt certain she was inside, that he was holding her hostage. I thought of the screams we'd thought we'd heard earlier and I thought of the smeared-out area on the clay tennis court and the dug-up area in the sand trap. *Jesus,* I thought, *what had this guy done? What had he done to someone else to cause them to scream like that? What did he have in mind for Alethea?*

I had to get inside the house, immediately.

I walked swiftly and furtively along the ridge of the roof. I was comfortable moving at these heights—I had worked on construction crews earlier in my life. I went all the way to the front of the house. I walked down to the right edge where I knew there was no window and sat there for a moment, listening. I heard some movement in the opposite corner of the house near the laundry room. I was right. Having seen me run behind the garage, he had gone looking for me near the laundry room window. I dropped my legs down over the corner of the roof and I grabbed onto the rain gutter. I hung for a moment to keep myself from swinging and I dropped down onto the lawn. I rolled as I landed so I would land with less noise.

I knew the basement door was on that side of the house. We didn't always lock it. We did if we thought of it, but we went in and out of that door at least a couple of times a week, taking out trash, and we often forgot to secure it. I went down the steps that led to the basement door and tried the knob. It turned. I eased the door open and went in, closing it and locking it as quietly as I could behind me. I crept up the stairs and stopped at the door that led into the kitchen. It was shut, but not latched. All the lights were out in the house, but I could still see, just barely, into the kitchen through the crack in the door. I crouched. I watched and listened.

Now this may not come as a surprise to you, but it did to me at that time. I heard, from behind the basement door, through the crack, the sound of Alethea speaking. She was on the phone, talking to the police.

"There's someone outside," she said. "I saw them running and then they went up on the roof, and now I don't know where they are."

She was calling from the kitchen phone. Except for the sound of her whispering, the house was perfectly silent.

"We thought we heard some screams and then I went out looking and now I think someone's trying to get in," she said.

I pushed open the basement door and came out into the kitchen.

"Will?" Alethea said. "Wilson!"

I still felt anxious, like the stalker was somewhere in the house. I felt we should be whispering, but Alethea said my name out loud. "Wilson? Was that you out there?" I realized that she understood me to be what she had been fearing.

"Oh my God, just a minute," she said out loud into the phone. "Oh my God, it's my boyfriend," she said to the police. "I think it was him I was hearing." She smiled, hunched her shoulders, and put her wrist to her forehead. She covered the phone.

"Was that you on the roof?" she said.

"It was," I said softly.

She smiled and shook her head.

"Sweet Jesus, Will," she said, putting the phone down and embracing me.

"Are you sure you're the only one in this house?" I said while she hugged me.

She looked over her shoulder and shrugged. "I think so," she said.

"Was that you that turned out the lights?" I asked.

"I was afraid. I saw someone running."

She quit hugging me, held her hands on the outside of my arms, and looked at my face. "Was that you running?" she said.

"Yeah, that was me."

She stepped back and put her wrist to her forehead again.

"I don't believe this. I can't believe it," she said, smiling.

"How long have you been in the house?"

"I had just gotten back," she said.

"Where were you?"

"I went out through the woods. Through the tennis courts."

"What in the hell were you doing?" I said.

"I was looking," she said, "for the cause of the screams."

I finally felt, at least somewhat, relieved.

"So it was you that I saw," I said, smiling, shaking my head. "When?"

"You came back, across the tennis courts?"

"Yes."

"Hunching over?"

"Yeah," she said, smiling shyly. "I was sneaking."

"Oh God," I said, rubbing my own forehead. "Yup, that was me on the roof," I said. I chuckled and shook my head.

"Are they still on?" I said, pointing at the phone on the kitchen table.

"Oh shit," she said. She picked up the phone and spoke into it. "Are you there? I'm sorry, hello?" she said, grinning at me. She listened and nodded. "Well, call off the dogs in that case, it was my boyfriend." There was a pause. "I don't know. I don't really know what he was doing on the roof, to tell you the truth," she said, smiling at me, "but it was definitely him. He's standing right here. I'm standing right here looking at him."

She squinted while she listened to whatever they were saying on the other end.

"Yeah, everything's fine. Would you say everything's okay, honey?" She held the phone out toward me so the officer could hear me speak.

"Yes, everything's okay," I said, projecting my voice for the first time since I'd been back in the house.

"Here, I'll give you to him," she said.

She handed me the phone. "Hello, Officer. Yes, everything's fine. I'm her boyfriend," I said.

"What were you doing on the roof?" the voice said.

I held the phone down and covered it with my hand. "He asked what I was doing on the roof," I said to Alethea, smiling.

"I'll be interested to hear," she whispered back.

"Well, Officer, I just got myself a little spooked, that's all. I thought I saw someone coming in toward the house."

"What were you doing outside?" the officer said.

"Well, I was chasing my girlfriend," I said, smiling at Alethea again.

"Chasing her?"

"I went out looking for her. Everything's fine, really."

The cop didn't speak, but I could hear his breathing.

"Seriously," I said. "No need to come out."

"We had someone all ready."

"Well, call them off, really."

"We'd be happy to come out and have a quick look around."

"It's not necessary," I said.

"Are you sure?"

"I'm positive."

"Okay." He was quiet for a couple of seconds, apparently thinking about something, and then he said, "You heard some screaming earlier?"

"Yeah, well, we thought we did." I thought for a moment myself. "How did you know we heard screaming?" I asked.

"Your wife told me," he said.

"Oh," I said, pausing. "My girlfriend."

"I guess, yes, your girlfriend. The woman that called," he said.

"It was probably some drunk people having a good time. Some drunk people coming out of the golf course is all," I said.

"I see," the cop said.

"We psyched ourselves out, that's all. I'm going to give you back to my girlfriend, to the woman that called you," I said.

I handed her the phone and she spent a few minutes reassuring him. "Yes, I'm sure, there's no one here but us. We just got all worked up. Don't bother coming out. Yes. Thanks a lot. We will. Goodbye," she said.

We sat down at the kitchen table and enjoyed a few more laughs about the whole thing. She made fun of me, laughed uncontrollably at the idea of me crawling in the sand trap on my elbows. I showed her the cut on my shin and she cooed over it a little, comforting me, but she couldn't keep from laughing at that, too. She guffawed when I explained how, swiftly and stealthily, I had scaled the wall, tiptoed across the garage roof, scaled the next gable, and scurried all the way to the front of the house.

"That roof is pretty steep," she said, buckling over.

"It's not too steep for me," I said, laughing myself. "I was like a Green Beret. I even took my shoes off."

"You did," she said, laughing, pointing at my feet.

"Shoes off for stealth," I said, letting her have her fun.

After a while she got up and poured herself some water and stood at the sink shaking her head and laughing some more. She tilted her neck back and drank making the same kind of loud gulping sounds that I had made earlier before any of this had occurred. I stared at the scar on her neck where she had had her first lump removed one year before.

"That manhunt made me thirsty," she said.

We stood there for a little while longer, relishing the humor, and then she said, "Well, I'm going up to bed." I was glad when she said this because, although I saw the comedy of the situation, I hadn't found it all quite as amusing as she had. I didn't tell her, but I still felt vaguely uneasy.

I made sure the back porch door was locked and I went around to all of the windows on the ground floor, making certain they were secure. I thought about the door in the basement, but I remembered that I had locked it behind me when I'd snuck in. I double-checked the front door and turned off all the lights downstairs.

When I got upstairs to the bedroom, Alethea had taken her clothes back off. She was sitting in bed with a pillow propped behind her, with her breasts exposed. In fact, all of her body was exposed. She didn't even have a sheet over her legs.

Without going into it too much, that time stands out to me more than any other time we made love. I tried to convince myself it was irrational, but I was still feeling like there was still a presence somewhere—in the house or outside—hearing what we were doing. Maybe that's part of what made it exciting.

She got very into it. She was incredibly loud, almost violent about it.

"Harder! Harder!" she kept saying. "Come on! I said *harder!*"

I felt like I was invading her, almost violating her.

After we were through, we lay there breathing heavily, feeling the cool air from outside come over our bodies. We didn't talk about it, but I'm sure I wasn't the only one listening for the strange noises again. I had left the fan off this time. I wanted to be able to hear everything clearly.

"You're not going to get up and leave if I fall asleep this time, are you?" I said.

She smiled affectionately. A cool breeze came in through the open window and blew over our bodies.

"Can I ask you a question?"

"Okay," she said.

"Why did you go out there without me?"

"I don't know," she said. She was silent for a moment. "I'm not really sure why I did. I wanted to see what was there, I guess. I wanted to see what was causing the screams."

"What were you going to do if you did find something?" I said.

"I don't know." She paused again. "I'm not sure." She sighed, and then she rolled over on her side and looked at my face.

"Let's rest now," she said, smiling warmly, touching my cheek, tucking my hair behind my ear. She draped her leg over mine and she cuddled up, nestling her chin into my neck.

I made sure she fell asleep first this time. Then, unable to relax, I lay there thinking back over everything. As I thought through it, I realized there were still a few things that didn't add up for me. I still wasn't clear on what was going on with the footprints. Were they just there from tennis players or golfers from earlier in the day? What were the smeared-out areas? Why was the sand trap partly dug out? Had someone from maintenance done that?

"Alethea," I finally said. "Were those your footprints on the tennis courts?"

She didn't wake up at first.

"Alethea, were those your footprints?" I said, touching her arm.

"What?" she said, half-asleep.

"Did you see the second set of footprints in the tennis courts . . . and the sand trap?"

She rolled over, touched the side of my face with her hand, and looked at me with drooping eyes. "Oh Wilson, go to sleep, darling," she said. "Forget about it."

The sex had made me a little bit drowsy. I felt like, if I could stop my mind, I would almost be able to sleep. After a few minutes, I got up and turned the fan back on. I lay back down and pulled the sheet up over my head. Soon I fell asleep.

I don't know how long I was sleeping this time either, but I know I awoke to a pounding. Someone was banging on the door downstairs.

I shook Alethea gently, but she didn't wake up right away. I shook her again.

"Someone's downstairs," I said. "They're pounding."

"What?" She sat up abruptly. "Who is it?"

The pounding came again. This was definitely real pounding, nothing imagined.

"What should we do?" she said.

I got up and went over to the bedroom window and peeked out. There was a police car in the driveway.

"It's the cops," I said. "They came anyway."

"We told them not to," Alethea said, lying back down.

I felt relieved it was them, but also annoyed.

"I knew this would happen. They're too bored not to come out," I said.

This was strange of me, I'll admit, but I was still very drowsy, half-asleep. I went downstairs without any clothes on. When I got to the bottom of the steps and flipped the light on, I became aware of my nakedness and I switched the light back off right away. I fig-ured, with the lights off in the house, I couldn't be seen. I planned to duck into the laundry room and grab a pair of shorts and a T-shirt from out of the dryer, where I knew I had clothes, but as I went through the living room and passed one of the windows, I noticed the shade was halfway up. I went over to it, to pull it down, and as I did, the light from a flashlight passed over my body. It came back and stopped on my crotch. I stepped away from the window. Standing away to the side, I put the shade down and then I stood there for a moment sighing, shaking my head. I peeked through the peephole on the front door. The cop was standing right there. I hurried into the laundry room and dug a pair of shorts and a T-shirt out of the dryer. I put them on and went back and flipped the front porch light on. I opened the door.

"We got a call about a disturbance," he said.

The officer was large, brawny. He was balding. He had taken off his hat and he was holding it in one hand. In the other he was grasping a Maglite. He had turned it off and he had slid his hand up to the end. He was gripping the Maglite like a billy club.

"This the right place, then?" he said.

He spoke in a rural Pennsylvania accent that was very familiar to me—a kind of Low German accent, partially inherited from the Amish in that area. His lips barely moved when he spoke. The words seemed to form from his throat.

"Yeah, we had called earlier," I said.

I rubbed my eyes trying to make it as obvious as I could that he had dragged me out of bed. I wanted to make it clear that that's why I had been naked.

He studied me.

"Sorry to be bothering you like this," he said.

Alethea came downstairs wearing a T-shirt and a pair of my boxer shorts. She appeared unusually pale.

The cop looked her up and down.

"It's kind of a formal thing, once the call's been made, we gotta check it out. You just can't know these days," he said, glancing back at me.

"Yeah?" I said.

"We just like to check on it." He paused. "We didn't mention it on the phone, but you just don't know."

"You don't know what, exactly?" I said.

He glanced at Alethea again and then he looked back at me. "Well, you pretty much gotta check it out, once the call's been made," he said. "They should've told youse on the phone." He paused again, watching her. "I mean, for all I know, it could be you," he said, fixing his eyes back on me. "You could be the one she's calling about. It could've been you on the phone, holding a gun to her head, making her tell us not to come."

"Yeah?" I said.

The officer hooked the Maglite in a ring on his belt and put his hat back on. He got a pen and a small notepad out of his shirt pocket.

"Now, you mind if I ask youse a few questions?"

I looked at Alethea. She raised her eyebrows.

"I guess not, go ahead," I said to him.

"Okay, what's your name, sir?" he said, peering at me over the notepad.

"Hues, Wilson Hues," I said.

"This your wife then here?"

Alethea was standing with her arms folded.

"He's my boyfriend," she said.

"Okay, ma'am. Your boyfriend. So youse ain't married." He paused. "Can I get your name?"

"Alethea, Alethea Shope," she said.

He scribbled on his pad.

"And what is your name, if I may ask?" Alethea said.

"I'm sorry?" he said.

"For all we know, it could be you," she said. "You could be the one causing those screams," she said.

"Okay, okay, I can see what you're saying," he said politely. "Youse want to see my badge or something?"

Alethea shrugged.

"My name is Paul Lutz. Officer Paul Lutz," the cop said. "What I'd like to do is ask you a few questions, that's all. Just a few questions is all," he said.

I glanced at Alethea. She just stared at him.

"Okay then." He flipped a page on his little notepad.

"This your house?" he said to me.

"It's *our* house," Alethea said.

"Okay, all right." He addressed the next question to her. "You two own it, then."

Alethea didn't say anything.

"We rent it," I said.

"And how long you been renting it?"

"Two months now," I said.

"Okay, two months," he said, scribbling. "And youse from here?" He protruded his lower lip outward after he spoke, gathering a bit of saliva that had gotten away from him.

"Yeah, I grew up nearby here," I said.

"In this neighborhood here?" he said.

Alethea sat down on the bottom step and stretched her shirt over her knees.

"No, I grew up south of town. On Reservoir Road," I said.

"Reservoir Road. Okay," he said. "And you, Miss Shope? You grow up there, too?"

"No," she said.

"Okay, okay. In town, then?"

"I'm not from here," she said.

That seemed to confuse him. He hesitated, staring at his notepad. He let rest the subject of her origins. "Well, I understand you heard some screams tonight," he said.

She nodded and shrugged.

"And someone was on your roof?" he said.

She shrugged and nodded again.

"That was me. It was me on the roof," I told him.

"It was you?"

"Yeah. We explained it on the phone," I said.

He stared at me, scratched the back of his pen on his balding head.

"I was searching for someone outside," I said.

"And did you find him?"

"No, not exactly," I said.

"You heard screams earlier, too. Is that right?"

"We thought we did."

"What did they sound like?"

"Like dying rabbits," Alethea said, smirking.

"Like dying rabbits?" he said, nodding.

"Yes, they sounded a little like dying rabbits. Strange screams," I told him.

"Okay," he said, addressing Alethea again. "And you been outside tonight, too?"

"Yes, I was," she said.

"Where you been?"

Alethea stood up, leaned on the banister, and crossed her arms again. She was bored and annoyed with him.

"Out back. I was out back looking around."

"And what were you looking for, ma'am?"

She hesitated.

"I'm not sure, exactly," she said.

"You're not sure?"

She stared at me and exhaled and then she looked back at the officer. He was waiting patiently.

"I was looking for whatever was causing the screams," she said, raising her eyebrows.

"Are you sure you heard screams?" he said a little too quickly.

Alethea peered at me. Her nostrils were flaring.

"I think I'm sure," she said.

We sat there in silence for five or ten seconds while he wrote on his notepad. He flipped up another page.

"And how long were you out there?" he said to her.

Alethea sighed and shifted her weight to her other leg.

"You know, I have to say," she said, sounding very defensive, "I guess I don't quite understand why *we're* being interrogated."

The officer put his pen in his shirt pocket and stared past both of us into the kitchen. He scratched his head again and he looked up at Alethea solemnly. "You know, ma'am, youse ain't the only ones that called tonight," he said.

We stared at him.

"We got another call from some other folks nearby here, about fifteen minutes after you did. They says they heared screams, too, but they says they was coming from your house. They says they seen some movement in your yard and later they heard screaming." He pursed his large lips and looked back and forth between the two of us. "We wasn't going to come out, but it got where we had to. You understand what I'm saying? Now, I'm just trying to work all this out myself. I'm just trying to establish some things here, in due process, is all, if youse don't mind cooperating."

Alethea had sat back down on the bottom step and propped her chin on her hands.

The cop addressed both of us. "Now. They said it was a woman's voice they heard."

I looked at Alethea. She rolled her eyes and exhaled.

"Yes, the neighbors heard a woman screaming in your house," he said.

I didn't want to be indicted for whatever else was going on outside, so I spoke up.

"That could have been us," I said.

He pulled his pen back out of his shirt pocket and got ready to write again. "Okay, it could have been you?" he said.

"It could have been her screaming," I said.

"Okay," he said eagerly.

"We were having sex," I told him.

Alethea stood up again at the foot of the steps. She was obviously very uncomfortable. She started shaking her head.

The cop observed her nervousness and then he started nodding and scribbling feverishly on his pad. The fact of our having had sex was apparently the missing link for him. He appeared suddenly satisfied.

"Okay, I see, okay," he said.

A strange burst came forth from Alethea. It was part exhale, part laughter.

"Phh. Well, I'm done with this. I'm going up to bed. I'm going to leave you with the *detective*," she said.

The officer seemed to regard this as a compliment. He looked up and nodded and then he started writing again. He was still scribbling when the bedroom door shut upstairs. He sucked his lower lip in and nodded.

"Well, I think I have enough here to go on," he said.

I stared at him.

"I guess I can leave you folks alone now," he said.

I was pleased that he was finally leaving our house. I wanted to get upstairs to make sure Alethea wasn't too upset.

I took the cop out the back door and we stood there on the porch for a few moments staring through the trees in the direction of the golf course. I had switched the outdoor lights back on on the way out and they were illuminating our back yard again. Once again, they lit up the first ten or twenty feet into the trees, but made the area beyond that very dark, very difficult to see.

"Looks like some rain coming in," the officer said, looking up at the sky and then at me.

The air did seem cooler. There was a slight breeze.

I remembered my shoes on the roof and I chuckled. The police officer watched me. It occurred to me that the evidence of my shoes on the roof might help corroborate our story.

"I think I'm going to hop up on the roof and get my shoes, so they don't get rained on," I said a little awkwardly.

"Okay, all right," he said.

Though I didn't ask him to, he walked with me around the side of the garage. He stood and watched while I stepped up on the chair, which was still against the wall, where I had left it. I pulled my chin up above the level of the roof so I could see the shoes. They were right there on the edge. It was a little difficult. I had to grab for each shoe quickly with one hand while holding on to the roof with the other. The first shoe landed on the ground, at the cop's feet. The second almost hit him. He had to hop out of the way, but he didn't seem offended. He even held the chair, stabilizing it as I let myself back down.

We walked over to his car in the driveway and he paused for a few moments.

"Well, I hope everything's under control here," he said.

"I'm sure it is," I said quickly.

He stared pensively back into the trees.

"You know, I want you to know, I don't think youse guys are crazy."

I watched him carefully as he spoke. He did the thing with his lower lip again, stretching it outward, gathering saliva that had strayed.

"I think it's very possible there was something out there tonight," he said, his eyes still fixed on the trees.

He waited for me to respond. I just stared at him.

He glanced off at the neighbors' home and he gazed up at the garage roof, where my shoes had been.

"You know, it's a tricky business. It's just tricky." He stared at me and shook his head. "I mean, how you supposed to know?" He looked in at the house, at the window on the back side of the house where our bedroom was, and then he looked off into the trees in the direction of the tennis courts. "You know they're there, but that ain't the hard part, the hard part is *finding* them." He paused, set his eyes on the trees again.

I watched him carefully.

"Seems like I spend half my life searching for intruders," he said.

I stared, myself, into the section of trees where he appeared to be staring. He was gazing wistfully, looking horribly troubled by whatever it was he hadn't found, by whatever it was he thought was in there but couldn't see. He kept gazing for what must have been a full minute. He seemed to forget I was even there.

"Well," I finally said.

"Well," he said, flinching, looking back at me. "Yes. Give us a holler if you need anything." He took a step toward his police car, paused, and looked at me for a few moments as if he was going to say something else—as if he was going to reveal something of great importance to me—but then he kept walking. I watched him open his car door, get in, and fasten his seat belt. He waved as he pulled out. I waited until he'd backed out of the driveway and driven out of sight, and then I went back into the house.

I locked the back door and I went to the front door where the cop had first come in, and I locked that, too. I went to the basement door where I had snuck in earlier, and even though I remembered locking it, made certain it was still secure. I checked a few of the windows that I had just checked and locked an hour before. When I got upstairs and opened the bedroom door, Alethea was curled up on her side, facing the opposite wall. She had the covers pulled up to her neck and she had her arm and leg draped over a pillow. I climbed in next to her. I left all my clothes on this time. I snuggled up behind her, also on my side, also facing the opposite wall. She had already fallen asleep, but she must have felt me crawl in. She scooched backwards, into me.

"I dreamed he came back again. He's not back again, is he?" she asked, half sleeping.

"No, I don't think so. It's just you and me here," I said.

Deer

The day after Alethea's funeral, I took off driving by myself. Somewhere in the Midwest, late at night, a deer darted out in front of my car and I hit it dead-on. Its forelegs were snapped in half and it was pushing with its hind end scraping along on the broken front legs with its hooves just dangling. It was trying to run, but it wasn't getting anywhere. Its eyes spun in their sockets and searched me when I came near. It occurred to me that the merciful thing was to put it away—to slit its throat or break its neck somehow—but I let it struggle there, even though I knew it had no real chance to live.

Perrito

Like so many other things, Alethea had gone out of my life. She had died on me. Her cancer had won.

I flew into Santiago and headed south from there. I had a week or two. I had the rest of my life.

In the hills of Viña del Mar, I chased eight condors from a crippled, dying lamb. Condors, as big as hyenas, opening its belly with their beaks.

"Leave it alone. Let it die in peace," I screamed, dispersing them.

Near the Neriguau River, I saw a field of bones. Clean white rib cages and vertebrae in a meadow, all in rows. It appeared as if they'd been arranged for death. Who had slaughtered the animals? Who had picked the carcasses clean?

In Patagonia, the land was ravaged by fire.

I saw a woman leaving flowers by a roadside shrine.

"What has happened to this land?" I asked her.

She spoke to me in English.

"It has burned," she said.

"When?"

"Many years ago."

"Who burned it?"

"The owners of the land," she said.

"They burned their own land?"

"*Sí*. They try to clear a space for themselves. The fires burn out of control, that is all," she said.

"Will anything grow again?" I asked.

"*Sí*, in time. In time it will be growing thick again," she said.

After a period of drifting, I settled on a little town on the central coast—a place I thought could soothe me for a number of days, perhaps weeks. It had fishermen, *artesanos,* and a humble, quiet bar with a rooftop veranda where I could drink alone and look out at the sea.

I took a cabana on the north end of the harbor. A pleasant elderly woman rented it to me. She spoke no English. Her face was weathered, wrinkled.

The little dog—the puppy, actually—was waiting outside the cabana. The woman looked at it and shook her head.

"*Ah, pobre perrito—tan pequeño y tan abandonado,*" the woman said.

She was right, it was much too young to be abandoned. It couldn't have been more than a few months old. It was severely emaciated. Its ribs and vertebrae were clearly visible. Behind its rib cage, its stomach was bloated disgustingly—doggie kwashiorkor, apparently. It also had a kind of mange disease. On half of its face and body, it had black fur, and on the other half, it was bald. On the bald areas, the pinkish skin was visible. Though it hadn't, I thought it looked like it had been burned, or treated with radiation.

As the elderly woman and I approached the dog, it laid its ears down in fear. The woman shook her head again, showing pity for a moment, but then she suddenly turned on it.

"*¡Fuera, perro! ¡Véte!*" She nudged it with her foot. "*¡Véte! ¿Busca tu mamá?*"

There were dogs everywhere in that country. One man, during my drifting, had told me that the government, twice a year, had extermination campaigns—that they went around the towns and cities and fed all dogs off of leashes steaks laced with cyanide.

The puppy hesitated as it walked off. It looked confused. I watched it as the woman led me into the cabana. She pulled back the curtain and swung open the window.

"*Con vista al mar,*" she said.

The dog had stopped and was staring through the cabana window.

"*Sí,*" I said.

"*¿Es muy bonita, no?*"

"*Sí,* very beautiful," I said.

"*Entonces. ¿Lo quiere? Es cincuenta mil pesos.*"

"*¿La cabaña?*" I said, staring out the window at the dog.

"*Sí, la cabaña.*"

"*Sí, la quiero.* I'll take it," I said.

That evening I got drunk alone and ate empanadas while staring out at the sea. The veranda was decorated with swords made from swordfish bills. The bartender took one off the wall and showed it to me.

"*Es de un pescado muy grande.* Is very big fish," he said. He told me that he had caught it, that he was very strong. "*Muy fuerte,*" he said, pointing to his bicep.

I watched his face for irony, but there was none.

Yes, you are very strong, I told him. "*Muy fuerte. Un hombre muy grande. Un pescado muy grande,*" I said, unimpressed.

Later in the evening, though my hunger didn't justify it, I ordered a stew with clams, mussels, and oysters. I can't remember if, when I requested it, I had the *perrito* in mind, but I do know that I thought of the dog a couple of bites into it. Once I had, I found it difficult to eat. I thought of the puppy's pink, mangy skin, its visible, bony shoulders, and its grotesque, bloated stomach, and the food lost its appeal for me. With considerable difficulty, I explained in my broken Spanish that I wanted a container to take the food out of the restaurant.

The waiter went in back and brought out the cook.

"*¿No le gusta?*" they asked.

I realized I was insulting them, but I insisted anyway.

"*Sí, me gusta, pero me la quiero llevar. Me la comeré más tarde,*" I said, with the dog in mind.

On the way home I passed a place with music blaring and people standing outside, drinking and laughing. There were foosball tables and Ping-Pong tables with young men heckling each other as they played. Young women clustered and whispered and smiled. Inside, there were rows and rows of old video arcade games. I stood over them for a while, gazing at the blinking lights, holding the styrofoam container of food. The attendant came over and asked me if I wanted to play. I gave him a coin and he smiled pleasantly.

"Juegue por cincuenta minutos," he said.

I played one of the old video games for a while, controlling the spaceship on the screen. The blinking lights had a numbing effect, made me forget myself for a while, but I soon grew aware again, felt restless. I went back outside where the Ping-Pong games were going on. I nearly forgot the food, but I remembered as I walked away that I had set it down by the video game. I went back and brought it with me outside.

I bought another beer and watched the young men play table tennis for a while. Eventually one of them asked me to play. I beat him in the first game and then, because the cluster of girls had been mocking him, he cheated me on the score. I picked up the styrofoam container of food and left.

I walked toward the northern tip of the harbor where the cabana was, staring out at the water on the way. There were rows and rows of boats beached on the shore. They were small wooden fishing boats, painted red and blue and green.

A couple of hundred feet past the boats, the beach disappeared. The water came all the way up to the dark, jagged rocks that formed the shoreline. I stopped and listened to the sound of the water crashing in, looked out at the white foam it made. After a few minutes, I continued up along the edge of the shore toward the little building that was, for a few days at least, my home.

I started looking for the little dog just outside the gate that led in toward my cabana. I looked around in the shrubbery, up and down the dirt path, but I didn't see the puppy anywhere. I looked down an outdoor corridor that led to the room where the elderly woman lived and I looked all around the entrance to my rental hut. I tried to convince myself that it was just as well, that I didn't want to get involved with the dog anyway, that it would only make it more difficult to leave.

I set the styrofoam container of food on a small table at the foot of my bed. I tried to go to sleep, but I had trouble dozing off. It was very hot so I got up and opened the windows. But then, with them open, I felt exposed. The cabana was on ground level and the bed was right next to the window. My imagination got the better of me, and before I knew it, I was imagining someone sneaking in the room holding a knife to my throat. That made me think of a friend whose family—many years before—had been stabbed to death. I tried to put all of that out of my mind just as quickly as it had come in. I listened to the sound of water on the rocks again, concentrated on the salty, cool air coming through the window over my body. Soon I was sleeping.

I don't know how late in the night it was. I don't know who the little dog was crying to—if it knew to come to the cabana and wail—or if it was just wailing to no one in particular, crying for itself, for the fact that it was lonely, thirsty, and starving. At first I thought I was having a kind of a nightmare. I may, in fact, have been. But then I was awake and there was the sound of the dog wailing. It was a very strange sound and if I hadn't recognized it— I had heard puppies in distress before, when I was very young—I might have thought it something that posed a threat to me. I had heard something like it many years before.

I was sleeping naked which I often do when I sleep alone. I fumbled around in the dark room for a few minutes to find my underwear. By the time I opened the door, holding the container of leftover seafood stew, the crying had stopped and the dog was gone. Perhaps I'd scared it away by the noise I'd made or perhaps I had scared it just opening the door. I looked up and down the dirt path outside the cabana and I peeked out the gate and searched along the water back where the games and the music had been, but there was nothing.

The wind had come up since I'd gone to bed, and the tide had apparently also risen. The water was higher on the rocks, crashing up more violently. Not knowing what name to call it by and not wanting to disturb the woman who had rented the cabana to me, I called and whistled, only very softly, for the dog.

"*Perrito, perrito,*" I said.

I don't know how that dog had the strength to run like it did— I don't know how it had the strength to do anything—but it came bounding out of some shrubs a hundred feet away. Truly, I didn't know healthy pups could run like that. This tiny dog was running in a way that seemed beyond it physically.

"*Ah, perrito,*" I said, crouching down as it approached.

It ran into my hands and it made little moaning sounds as I petted it. Oddly, almost unbelievably, it didn't try to tear open the container of food, which I had set down on the ground next to me. It knew it was hungry—it certainly knew that—but it also knew that it was lacking all of the things a parent should provide it with. I put my hand near its tiny snout and it started to suck on my finger as if it was a nipple. I don't think this little dog had eaten any solid food at all since its mother had abandoned it.

I thought of picking the pup up, to comfort it, but at this point I was still fighting myself, trying to keep a kind of distance from it. Also, it was very dirty, very grotesque. Just petting it, I could feel its bony skull and I could feel its ribs protruding. I was afraid that if I picked it up, I would somehow injure it.

I opened the styrofoam container and the puppy thrust his

nose in. He started making the moaning sounds that he had made a few moments earlier when I had first petted him—sounds not unlike the ones a human baby makes when drinking from its mother's breast.

"*Hmm, hmm, hmm,*" the dog went.

He ate feverishly, chewing the soft bodies of the shellfish, swallowing them only when he could muster the strength to squeeze them through his little esophagus. His gums must have been tender, so he couldn't accomplish much by chewing. Mostly he lapped at the stew as if it were milk.

You may know this about dogs. Even your own pet, if you approach it while it's eating, will growl at you. Certainly dogs like the dogs in Chile—homeless, semi-wild strays, fending for themselves—behave this way. But this little dog didn't do any of that. I don't think it was old enough to have learned that if it was going to live, it was going to have to *fight* for its own survival. I don't think it comprehended its own abandonment.

I petted it while it ate.

After a while, I went inside and searched for a container to put water in. There were no cups, and the water bottle I had in my backpack was nothing the puppy could drink from. In the bathroom, I found that the soap dish was a clam shell. I rinsed it as thoroughly as I could—so the dog wouldn't taste the soap—and I drew some water into it. By the time I carried it out to him, he was nearly finished with the liquid part of the stew. He had eaten around most of the solid pieces, and now that they were the only things left, he was aggressively chewing on the sinewy bodies of the shellfish, trying to swallow them.

"*Perrito, bebe. Agua,*" I said.

I watched him eat some more.

"*Necesitas agua también.* Water," I told him. "Drink."

It only occurred to me as I watched him struggle to chew the more solid food in the stew that there was a very good chance this dog would get sick from the food. I remembered hearing stories of starving people—people with kwashiorkor—dying even after food arrived because their bodies rejected it. There was a risk that this dog would vomit all of the nourishment.

"*Para, perrito. Ya comiste mucho,*" I said.

The dog followed the plate and kept eating off of it as I pulled it away, but once again, he didn't growl or show his teeth or protest. He just looked up at me, licking the remaining flavor off his snout, wagging his tail gratefully.

I put down the half clam shell of water in place of the food and he started lapping it up just as eagerly. I refilled the shell two or three times, each time petting him as he drank. His skin felt old and rough for a young dog. It had a leathery texture where the mange had taken over, where he had no fur. I thought of bringing him in the room with me, but I decided against it. I thought, *No, this dog must not become accustomed to this. He must not become dependent on humans for warmth and food or else, when I leave, he will surely starve.*

I brought a towel from the bathroom and spread it out in the dirt, in front of the cabana door. The puppy came right into it. He walked in a circle, as dogs do to make their beds, and then he lay down in it. I folded the towel like a blanket, up over him so that just his nose and face were peeking out.

"*Qué lindo perrito.* Cute *perrito,*" I said to it.

I scratched it on the head, scratched its pink, hairless flesh, and it panted with its tongue out.

I had trouble falling asleep that night. I was sure I'd wake up to the puppy's wails, to it vomiting, or worse, I was afraid I'd sleep through the cries and wake up to its lifeless corpse outside my door. As I lay in bed trying to fall asleep, I tried to convince myself that I had done everything I could. I tried to convince myself that if it died, it would die full, happy, and warm. That was, after all, more than could be said for most humans.

The next morning, when I awoke and looked, the dog was gone. I went out into the courtyard and looked up and down the dirt road, out onto the beach, but I didn't see it anywhere. I wasn't sure what to think. I wasn't sure if it had gone off to die somewhere, or if I should take the fact that it had gotten up and left as a good sign. Then I realized that the towel I had put out for it was gone. The elderly woman who had rented me the hut had probably run the dog off again.

I dressed and walked to the edge of the water, to the beach, and headed up toward the other end of the harbor where I had eaten and drunk the night before. I came upon the *perrito* curled up, peacefully, in the sand. At first I was afraid that it was dead. I went up to it and put my hand on its rib cage. Its diaphragm was moving up and down. The dog awoke and sniffed and licked my hand. It hopped to its feet.

"*Perrito, vamos,*" I said.

The dog followed me up the beach, wagging its tail. We walked down to the section of beach where the red and green and blue fishing boats landed. Most of them were out on the water, but five or six had already returned from their early-morning fish harvests. There were *caballeros,* men on horses, helping drag the boats up out of the shallow surf onto the dry beach. Women and children and old men sat in rows untangling the trotlines. They were taking minnows off of hooks, examining them and deciding, with each tiny fish, whether to discard it or preserve it for the next fishing day. Two men in yellow rain slickers were cleaning fish, selling the fillets to townspeople.

"¿Pescado para el perrito?" I said.

I thought I might teach the puppy where it could get scraps so it could survive after I was gone.

"Para el perrito que tiene hambre," I said, but the men in the jackets cleaning the fish and the townspeople buying fillets from them just stared at me.

I tried this same thing at a couple of the trotline detangling stations where they were sorting—and, I thought, discarding—minnows, but the people just gazed at me like I was crazy. They must have thought I was very strange—perhaps insane—for trying to help that stray.

We didn't scrounge up any food that morning, the *perrito* and I, but we did have a pleasant stroll around the harbor. He romped after me, followed me all the way back up to the north end, past my cabana, to the dilapidated pier where the artisans had set up little stations to sell their crafts. I browsed for a half-hour or so, bought some purple earrings for my mother back in the States. I bought myself a gift or two also. I bought a rock with an image of an old man carved into it. The old man was reaching up to the heavens in desperation.

"¿Qué es esto?" I asked the man who had carved it.

"Qué es . . . es un hombre desperado . . . tratando de alcanzar la mano de Díos."

"¿Donde está la mano de Dios?" I asked. I didn't see anything that looked like the hand of God in the carving.

"No. No hay," he said.

On the way back to the cabana, the puppy and I came upon a couple of dogs fighting over a fish carcass. They were growling at one another, jockeying for position. One of them looked to me like it could be the *perrito*'s parent. Where it had fur, it had the same black fur as the puppy. It had mange and it had a similar kind of leathery, pinkish skin. It had the same thin snout, the same long, skinny legs.

It escaped the other two dogs with a nice piece of meat—most of what there was of the carcass—and it chomped only two or three times before swallowing it. When it was through licking its lips, I went over and looked at it. The dog was unhealthy—too thin, no doubt—but it certainly looked stronger and healthier than the *perrito*. I looked for breasts on the dog, but I saw that it was male. I had already been feeling anger toward it, suspecting it was the puppy's parent. When I saw that it was male, I felt furious. I picked up the puppy carefully—I was still worried about hurting its frail body—and I carried it over to the big, mangy dog who had, by now, lain down on the beach, satisfied from its meal of fish.

"*¡Tu niño!*" I said. "*¡Comprende!*" I put the puppy up to its nose so it would have to recognize the smell, so it would have to reckon with the truth of its having abandoned its own young. "*¿Comprende?*" I said.

The puppy nestled its nose in near the adult dog's belly, apparently looking for teets. The big dog, the father, sniffed at the *perrito* and then it lumbered to its feet, in a lazy kind of way, and sauntered off down the beach.

It was low tide and we were standing on the sand next to the rock wall where the water had been crashing up the night before. For the puppy to get up and over the rocks back up to the dirt path where my cabana was, I'd have to carry it. I climbed up on the rock wall and stood there watching the little dog to see what it would do, to see if it would try to follow me. The pup looked at me for a moment and then, to my surprise, despite the fact that the adult dog had just rejected it, it went trotting off down the beach after its father. I felt—momentarily, irrationally—hurt that the *perrito* was leaving me, but then I checked myself. *Don't be ridiculous,* I thought. *This is good. Maybe the father will show the* perrito *some places to forage for food, maybe it will teach the puppy how to struggle for its own sustenance.*

I spent one more evening in that town. I had beer and empanadas again, looked out at the water in the same way that I had the night before. I bought seafood chowder for the pup this time—a cream-based soup which, I thought, was more like the milk that his digestive system was accustomed to. He was sleeping by my door when I got in. I wrapped him in a T-shirt this time— my own T-shirt, so the woman wouldn't take it away.

The next morning the little dog was gone again. My T-shirt was still there. I went out on the beach and looked down toward the boats, up toward the pier where the *artesanos* were set up again, but I didn't see it anywhere. *Maybe the pup is getting stronger now,* I thought. *Maybe this is a favorable sign.*

I ate breakfast on a screened-in porch that was attached to the home of the old woman who'd rented the thatched hut to me. I had skipped breakfast the day before, but it came with the room and I decided to cash in on it. She didn't say anything when she brought me the eggs, toast, and Nescafé. I ate without speaking to her. I stared out at the beach, looking for the dog. When I had finished eating, she scolded me for befriending it.

"*Este perro es peligroso. Tiene una infección.* Is dangerous," she said. She pretended to itch her arms. She told me that I had made a mistake. That now the dog would keep coming around.

After breakfast, I sat under a thatch umbrella on an uncomfortable wooden chair and tried to figure out what to do. I was starting to feel very restless. A fog had moved in over the *pueblito.* The little wooden fishing boats were coming and going in the harbor.

I tried to convince myself that it was okay to leave. I considered taking the pup along, but when it was time for me to leave the country, I wouldn't be allowed to take it with me anyway. If I carried it on my journey and then left it in another part of Chile, it would have an even smaller chance to live. The best thing, I decided, was to leave it in this *pueblito.* There was nothing more I could do for it. I had gotten too involved anyway. I had done what I could. It was just an animal. I needed to move on.

There was a sign I had seen on the edge of town for a beach, for a *playa.* I had already paid the woman the night before, so I was free to leave without speaking to anyone. It was a good time to go. The *perrito* wasn't around. I could get out of town without it seeing me leave.

I gathered up my things, put my backpack on, and started out of town, but I couldn't stop thinking about the little dog. Five or ten minutes into the walk on the dirt road that led out of town, I decided to go back and look for it again. One last time. One last meal could make the difference for it, I decided.

I walked back and I went onto the beach among the fishing boats in the area where I had tried to get it scraps the morning before. I walked up the beach where I had seen the dog curled up the day before. I looked around the cabana, in and around the shrubs where it had been hiding a few nights before. I asked the woman I had rented the cabana from.

"*¿Sabe donde esta el perrito?*"

"*No, no sé,*" she said.

I walked up among the *artesanos* and asked the man I had bought the rock carving from.

You have seen the little dog? I asked him, in Spanish.

"¿Cuál perrito?"

"El perrito del ayer."

He thought for a moment.

"¿Es tu perrito?" he said.

"Más o menos."

"No, no sé," he said.

I walked back up and found the men in yellow jackets who I had asked for scraps.

"You've seen the *perrito*?"

They looked at one another and laughed.

"¿Perrito? ¿Cuál perrito? Hay perros en toda la playa," they said.

I gave up. I started walking, south and east, out of town.

A man on horseback came up behind me. It was one of the caballeros who had been helping pull the boats up onto the beach.

"Hola," he said, nodding.

"Hola," I said.

He kept looking at me as if he expected me to ask him an important question.

"Sabe donde está . . ." I considered asking him about the dog. *"¿Donde está la playa?"* I said. "The *beach*?"

He thought for a moment.

"¿Cuál playa?" he said.

"Cualquier playa. Una playa . . . bonita," I said.

The horse tried to move forward and he pulled back on the reins.

The beach season is over, he told me in Spanish. *"¿Por qué quiere ir a la playa?"*

"No sé. Porque quiero ver una cosa bonita."

"¿Una cosa hermosa?" he said, nodding solemnly. You realize there is no sun on the beach, he told me. *"No hay sol hoy,"* he said.

I realize, I don't need to have sun, I told him, nodding.

He explained to me that it was fall and that the fog had come in in that region. He said that if he took me there, the beach would be heavy on my eyes, heavy on my eyes and my spirit. *"Muy pesado en sus ojos y espíritu,"* he said.

"Quiero ver." I want to see. I want to go anyway, I said.

Of course. You are a wise man. *"Un hombre inteligente. Por supuesto. La playa es bonita cuando está nublado. Tienes razón. Muy hermosa,"* he said.

I rode with him on the back of his horse down a tiny dirt path that turned off of the bigger road where cars sometimes passed. There was no saddle on his horse, only a bridle, reins, and a folded blanket. I tried to brace myself on the animal, with my hands behind me, but I didn't feel stable. I was forced to hold on to the waist of this man whom I had just met.

The path led into a wooded area. We rode in silence. Soon I had the sense we were ascending. We came out of the trees to a magnificent pinnacle hundreds of feet above the beach and the ocean.

"Here we dismount the horse," he said, now speaking English. "Here we sit among the rocks and look out at the beautiful, tireless ocean."

"You speak English," I said.

"Yes, perhaps I do. Perhaps I speak many languages. Perhaps I am wise about many things," he said smugly.

We got off of the horse, one at a time, and he led me down onto the rocks. It was a steep embankment, but it wasn't so steep that we couldn't climb down it, down onto the rocks that it was made up of. We came to rest on a large boulder with a smooth area that was comfortable to rest on. From somewhere beneath his *ponchilla,* he pulled out a flask, drank from it, and passed it to me. I drank from it also. It was a kind of wine—both sweet and bitter in my mouth. It was warm in my belly.

"I come here when I have sadness," he said. "Here, my sadness turns into beauty."

I was beginning to feel trust for him. *This man is wise, like a good father,* I was thinking. "You see? The fog has come in," he said.

It had. Sitting up on the pinnacle, everything—the beach, large shoals jutting up out of water off the shore, the *pueblito* to the north—was barely visible through the dank mist.

"*Señor,*" the man said. "I have seen you these days. I have seen you these days with the *perrito.*"

I felt for a moment like I had been caught.

"*Sí,*" I said.

"What are your plans for the dog?" he said.

"I have no plans for it," I said.

"Then why were you feeding it?"

I considered the question carefully.

"Because it was hungry," I told him.

"Perhaps the dogs in this country, you are finding them different than the dogs where you come from?"

I paused, looked off at the ocean.

"Do you understand what I'm saying?"

The man was losing his patience with me.

"*Amigo,*" he said, "is it possible for you to take the dog with you where you are going?"

He had been sitting on the rock with his knees drawn up to his chest and his hands locked around the front. He stretched his legs out, stared out at the water, and rested his hands on his lap.

"Tell me, how many days you were in the village?" He gestured south of us, to the *pueblito.*

"*Dos días,*" I said.

"*Dos días. Dos días,*" he said, nodding. "And tell me this." He spoke sternly. "Tell me this, young man. If you can feel affection for a dog in two days, what does it mean for your human affections?" He paused. "You must learn to manage your love. A man must manage his affections. You must learn to be a man. You must learn the mercy of ruthlessness."

I looked out at the ocean, at the water splashing up over the rock jetties and shoals. I looked at the little town where I could see the fishing boats coming and going again. I looked south, beyond the town, at the mountains. They were just visible in the fog, the layers and layers of peaks, soft undulations.

"*Bueno,* then I will never be a man," I told him, climbing up out of the rocks.